The Diary
of
Thirty 84

PERFECTION

CHAPTER 1

JOURNAL ENTRY
JANUARY 21ST

I always dream about my mother. When the alarm goes off, she's moving her legs in slow motion, leaning back to avoid the waves. I don't notice, but I also *do* notice. Because as her leg lifts, it pushes sand into my newly dug hole.

Every morning, the alarm wakes me up. It's sudden, repetitive, and it screeches. In case anyone finds this, my name is Cynthia 3084. But I like to say "Thirty 84". It feels more creative. Less like a number, more like a person.

I'm a mix of metal and flesh, or what we call a cyborg. For now, I can't tell how much is metal and how much is flesh. But I know my eyes are deep puddles of emotion, and I know there's a part of me that's human.

My life is defined by routine. Mornings: Stretches, back stretches, waist stretches, leg stretches. Breakfast: a scrambled egg, a tablespoon of peanut butter, green tea. I end the morning with strength training exercises: a 10-pound weight in each hand.

Outside, the skyscrapers loom above, flashing digital advertisements. We live in an ordered, rhythmic, and coordinated world. There are no honking horns, no speeding cars. Our world is robotic and futuristic.

Public transport arrives exactly on time, each autonomous vehicle gliding silently to its destination, powered by an unseen energy grid beneath the surface.

Parks are filled with sculpted greenery, their perfect symmetry designed by AI botanists who know the exact ratio of flora to optimize air quality and aesthetics. The air is clean, crisp, and engineered.

*

I walk to work every day, passing the same group of cyborgs in black coats. We all dress the same. Male cyborgs in one uniform: a black one-piece suit. Female cyborgs in another: a white one-piece suit. Unless you're up close, the male cyborgs are indistinguishable from each other. The same goes for us females. The uniformity is deliberate, of course. Designed for efficiency.

The suits highlight the precision of our enhanced bodies: streamlined and sculpted, with no unnecessary bulk. The material absorbs light without reflection, giving male suits a matte finish, while the female suits shimmer faintly in the right light, a subtle nod to distinction. Even our coats, long and angular, are engineered for efficiency. They adjust to the temperature and are resistant to every imaginable element. In this city, difference is a design flaw. Perfection demands conformity, and perfection rules us all.

*

The office. It's sterile. Cyborgs at desks. Typing. It's redundant work. We sit at our stations, typing in what feels like unison. The faint clicking of keys creates a mechanical rhythm. No one speaks. There's nothing to say.

My job is to write and edit articles for the city. Except nothing happens. Or, rather, nothing worth reporting. My articles cover the city's "progress": the installation of new turf in the park, the exact amount of rain we received last week, or the efficiency of the latest AI-driven transport update. Every word is polished, approved, and utterly devoid of substance. It's a well-oiled loop: the mundane packaged as news, reinforcing the illusion of perfection. Anything violent—executions, recycling of cyborgs—is never reported. We witness it, we know about it, but there are never statistics or reports on who was executed or who was recycled. It becomes word of mouth, only. We absorb the disappearances, process them silently, and move on. That's what we're programmed to do.

In my case, I like to make every redundant day a little different.

I sit at my desk, the same as every other desk. My to-do lists hover, sharp and clinical, before dissolving into my list of tasks for the day: write an article about the pristine upkeep of the city's artificial lakes. Edit a press release on the rising efficiency metrics in energy redistribution.

The monotony claws at me, but I channel it into

small acts of defiance. I rearrange the sentence structure in my articles, breaking the perfect rhythm just enough to feel different. I take an extra second to type a word, letting my fingers linger on the keys. It's minuscule, imperceptible, even, but these small differences are mine.

The green light from the camera blinks, a constant reminder of my place in this machine. But it can't see my thoughts. It doesn't know how I try, in tiny, invisible ways, to feel alive.

My routine continues.

CHAPTER 2

On the wall, a digital clock blinks, its steady rhythm a metronome for our lives. A robotic voice interrupts our typing: "One minute to lunch." The room remains silent except for the keyboards, fingers moving in a synchronized clatter. I finish my story, "*Traffic Report for Monday*," just as the bell goes off.

It's lunchtime. We rise in unison, chairs sliding back with precision. No one hesitates, no one lingers. We move as a single stream toward the hallway and into the cafeteria. It's a seamless process.

In the cafeteria, the layout never changes. There are three stands, stark and uninviting: **Vegetables, Protein, Carbohydrates.** The signs glow softly, listing items that are as bland as they are predictable. The higher-ups strongly encourage we take one portion from each stand. No deviations. No substitutions. Every tray looks identical.

I collect my rations and head toward my usual spot. Every lunch, I sit with two co-workers I met years ago: Pinal and Sean. They're both cyborgs, of course, but they still have something that feels... different. They talk a lot, more than any cyborg I know. Their words tumble over each other, a constant stream of observations, jokes, and stories.

I rarely contribute, but I like their company. There's a comfort in their voices, a rhythm that drowns out the sterile monotony of our existence. I sit there, chewing on my uniform meal, and let their chatter distract me. For a few moments, I can almost forget the clock on the wall, the cameras in the corners, and the endless routine that defines our lives.

Today Pinal eyes me with an intensity. "What?"

His eyes narrow. "I said, do you wanna come to the recycling event?"

"Event?"

His mouth falls open slightly. Bits of food dangle from the corner. "You don't know what the recycling event is?" Pinal shoots a look over at Sean. "She doesn't know what the recycling event is."

Sean doesn't look up. "Recycling. Cyborgs."

Ah, yes. Of course. *That.* I nod. Pinal coins new terms all the time.

A silence as Pinal looks at me, waits. "So, do you wanna go?"

Sean shakes his head. I shake mine. Sean looks up finally, over at Pinal. "Why are you so overenthusiastic?"

Pinal snorts. "Cuz I love that kind of shit. It's like watching fucking cars getting scrapped."

"I wouldn't compare recycling to watching cars getting scrapped," I add.

Sean chimes in. "It's more like watching an execution."

Pinal blurts out, almost angrily. "No, cuz they have actual executions. I've been to one."

Pinal never surprises me, but this surprises me. "Why did you go to an execution?"

Pinal smiles. "Cuz I fucking love that kind of shit."

CHAPTER 3

JOURNAL ENTRY
JANUARY 22ND

When I pass an advertisement for a "*recycling*," I stop. The holographic display projects an older cyborg volunteering to be recycled. Beneath it, the text reads: **"For the Betterment of Society."** The message is persuasive, as if the process were a noble act. But no amount of sterile language can mask what it truly is.

We were told that recycling and executions would create a perfect society. That eliminating the elderly (recycling) or the dysfunctional (executions) would prevent overpopulation and contribute to a well-run society. Perfection, they said, requires sacrifice.

And so, we obeyed. We believed that with enough refinement, enough recycling and executions, the paranoia of who would be next would fade. Instead, it lingers, like a thick, invisible smog.

We work so hard to distinguish ourselves from humans. Our enhanced bodies, free of disease and fatigue. Our minds, rid of emotion-driven decisions. Our efficiency, unmatched. Yet, when I see the crowds gather at a recycling event or an execution, I feel the shadow of something hauntingly familiar. Humans once had public executions. Spectacles that drew crowds, hungry for entertainment or justice, depending on how you looked at it. This feels no different.

And yet, as I stand there, watching the hologram flicker with its false promises of perfection, I feel it. The same unease I imagine humans felt centuries ago. The same distrust. The same fear. We're supposed to be above this, beyond the primal instincts that governed human societies.

We may look perfect. We may function perfectly. But our paranoia of imperfection is as human as it gets. And no amount of executions will ever purge it.

*

My evenings are my favorite part of the day. It's the only time that feels like mine. No directives, no quotas, no cameras watching my every move. It's when I indulge in my "passion," though even calling it that feels like a rebellion.

Every night, I watch documentaries on humans. I'm fascinated by their lives, their chaos, their flaws. I've seen grainy footage of protests, lovers holding hands in the rain, mobs attacking strangers. Their emotions are unrestrained, raw, spilling out of them with a kind of reckless abandon that I almost envy.

And then there's the banging. The familiar, jarring sound echoes through the wall I share with my neighbor, Don. Don 0773. His job is data entry. Mundane, soul-crushing work. Typing strings of numbers into his terminal day after day. It drives him insane, and every so often, in a burst of frustration, he bangs his head against the wall.

I don't blame him. I feel it, too. That crushing weight of monotony. The kind of emptiness that creeps in when every aspect of your life is dictated for you. What our perfect society didn't account for was that in eliminating all imperfections—passions, relationships, intimacy, even sex—it also erased the very things that made life worth living.

We're not allowed to love. We're not allowed to connect. Even friendships are shallow, more about convenience than companionship. The result? We're bored. Our lives, while efficient, lack color. I sit in my perfectly ordered apartment every night, watching imperfect humans with a longing I can't fully explain.

Don's head against the wall sends a jarring vibration through my apartment. It's unnerving, but I've never had the heart to tell him to stop. How could I? I understand it too well. I feel the same suffocating frustration that drives him to it, the same hollow ache of monotony that pushes him to try, however futilely, to feel something, anything.

Once, in a rare moment of interaction, I knocked on his door. I had run out of butter. He invited me in, his face a blank mask, the same as mine, yet something in his eyes felt... off. Angry. Disdainful.

His computer sat against our shared wall, a harsh light in the darkish room. Lines and lines of numbers filled the screen, scrolling endlessly like a digital waterfall. I remember standing there, staring at them, unable to look away. It was hypnotic, almost beautiful in a way, yet horrifying. This is his life. This is what he does, all day, every day. Just types numbers into a system, over and over. No variation, no deviation. His entire existence boiled down to an endless stream of digits.

That's why, when he bangs his head against the

wall, I don't get angry. I don't knock back to tell him to stop, even when it interrupts my documentaries. I just turn up the volume, letting the narrator's voice drown out the thumping. It's easier that way.

Tonight, I'm watching a war documentary called *Santiago Files*. It's about humans and the violent conflicts they waged. The footage is grainy, flickering with explosions and chaos. The narrator's voice is calm, almost reverent, as he describes the rise of cyborgs.

"Cyborgs are a more evolved species," he says over the images of tanks rolling through rubble. "Level-headed, able to build a society without being consumed by hatred, greed, anger, mental issues, depression…"

His words linger, hanging in the air like a thin layer of frost. I press pause, letting the screen freeze on a haunting image of an army tank moving through the streets. The narrator's words replay in my mind. Hatred, greed, anger. Those were flaws, sure. But they were also fuel. They drove humans to create, to fight for what they believed in, to feel something deeper than programming.

The narrator leaves out the most important part of what makes humans unique: passion. The chaos they lived with, the emotions that tore them apart, were also what made them whole. Passion gave them art, love, dreams. It gave them a reason to live beyond efficiency and order.

I think of Don and his numbers. I think of his head banging against the wall, his silent rebellion. I think of myself, watching human lives play out on my screen every night, yearning for something I can never fully name.

The narrator's voice tells me we're better. More advanced, more evolved. But if that's true, why does it feel like we've lost so much?

*

The screeching alarm again. Sharp, piercing. Like every other morning. Another routine, another monotonous script: breakfast, exercises, walking to work. The city feels subdued today, blanketed in an overcast sky.

At work, I don't bother looking towards the window. There's no light to bathe in, no moment of stolen joy. Instead, I decide to take a bathroom break, not out of necessity, but for the rare chance to simply... think.

The bathroom is one of the few places where silence feels almost tolerable. But even here, there's a camera mounted in the corner, silently observing. I know it's there to ensure we stay efficient, to ensure we don't linger too long or show any signs of rebellion. The thought of it unnerves me, but there's nothing for the footage to report. Sitting on a toilet is as mundane as it gets. Unless, of course, you sit for too long. That, too, could be flagged. Even moments of idleness are monitored, scrutinized.

I sit there, staring at the floor. Every day feels like this. An endless repetition of tasks, moments, and feelings that blend together into an indistinguishable haze. My life, like Don's, feels like a string of numbers: precise, predictable, and utterly devoid of meaning. I stare at the white tiles on the floor, searching for something, anything, to break the monotony. But I know the truth.

Nothing will change unless I change it.

CHAPTER 4

JOURNAL ENTRY
JANUARY 28TH

We're not allowed to be in the human neighborhood, and humans are not allowed to be in ours. The rules are clear and absolute. We're kept separate, their chaos a direct contrast to our perfection. Cyborgs are forbidden from witnessing their "passions": their drinking, gambling, sex activities, or drug addictions. These are labeled "human flaws," the vices that held them back and justified our creation. Yet, despite the warnings, I find myself drawn to it all. The rawness of their lives, the unfiltered imperfection that we've been engineered to reject.

At night, when the streets are quiet, I take long walks along the border of our neighborhoods. Sometimes, when I'm sure I won't be noticed, I slip inside. It's a world so different from ours, a place that feels alive in ways our pristine city never could. The streets are grungy and dilapidated, the buildings cracked and leaning like they're on the verge of collapse. Overflowing trashcans line the sidewalks, their contents spilling onto the streets. Potholes make the roads uneven, forcing cars and bikes to weave through them like dancers improvising a routine.

And yet, their neighborhoods pulse with life. People move through the streets, shouting, laughing, arguing, crying. It's messy, loud, and unpredictable. We have perfection. They have chaos. But I like it here better.

When I come here, I'm nervous, always on high alert. My eyes dart to every shadow, every movement, but beneath the anxiety, there's a strange, forbidden happiness. It's like stepping into another world, a world that feels real in a way mine never has.

A man in a cowboy hat, shorts, and cowboy boots rummages through a trashcan, muttering to himself. His hat is worn, the brim bent and frayed. When he notices me, he stops and tips his hat. His eyes are sad. "I lost all my money in the crash," he says, his voice tinged with resignation.

I don't know what to say. We don't deal in pleasantries or small talk in my world. I nod instead, an awkward acknowledgment, and keep walking. His eyes linger on me for a moment before he goes back to sifting through the trash.

Up ahead, under the dim glow of a streetlamp, a woman stands waiting. Her fishnet stockings cling tightly to her legs, and her red dress, slightly torn at the hem, seems to reflect the light. She shifts her weight from one foot to the other, looking around with sharp, nervous eyes. A man approaches her. They exchange a few quiet words, their conversation quick and transactional. Then, they walk away together, disappearing into the shadows of a nearby alley.

This is prostitution: the forbidden deed in our world. In ours, intimacy is a distant memory, replaced by efficiency and control. Relationships are obsolete, rendered unnecessary by our perfection. But here, in this run-down human neighborhood, emotions are raw and unapologetic. It's messy, flawed, and stripped of any

15

pretense.

As I walk further, I wonder if this is what I've been searching for all along. Not the act itself, but the emotion behind it. The desperation, the longing, the connection. These people, for all their flaws, are alive in ways we've been taught to forget. And as much as I fear getting caught, as much as I know I don't belong here, I keep coming back. Because in their chaos, I find a glimpse of what it means to be free.

*

When I go back home, I think about the prostitute, the act of selling your body for sex. How it feels, whether passion ever enters the equation.

As I lie in bed, my thoughts spiral, tangled between the world I live in and the one I keep sneaking into. The prostitute's face looms large in my mind, her eyes meeting mine from the shadows, beckoning me. Her smile is slow, deliberate. It's a smile that promises something unknown, something forbidden.

Then, her laughter comes, harsh and cackling, amused by my innocence. It rings in my ears, mingling with the shrill sound of my screeching alarm, dragging me back to the reality I've been trying to escape.

It's time to wake up.

CHAPTER 5

When I go to work, two male cyborgs watch me as I enter the building. It's possible that I'm imagining this. A projection of paranoia in my mind, a fleeting moment of insecurity. But I'm not. I can feel their gaze, sharp and assessing, as if they're not just observing my actions but studying me, measuring something deeper.

One of those cyborgs stands by the door, his posture rigid, like he's been programmed to stand there. His hair is slicked back into a tight ponytail, and his hawkish features are frozen in a perpetual expression of intense focus. He never looks away. As I pass him, I feel his eyes following me in a way that's... deliberate. He continues talking with his companion, his voice low and steady, but his eyes never leave me. The other cyborg, a bit thinner, holds a suitcase, glancing at me only for a second before returning his attention to their conversation. But the first male cyborg, his eyes are locked on me, unblinking, and I can feel the weight of it, even as I try to push it from my mind.

By the time I step into the building, I'm already unnerved. The walls feel closer, the lights brighter, and for a brief moment, I wonder if my every move is being tracked. It's a sensation I can't shake, like I'm more than just another cyborg here, like I'm under some kind of scrutiny. The doors close behind me with a soft hiss, and I try to breathe. It's nothing, I tell myself. Just another glitch in the system.

*

At lunch, with Sean and Pinal, I sit in silence. The usual banter bounces around the table. Sean talks about some new upgrade he's seen, Pinal laughs at a joke I didn't hear. Their words wash over me, but my mind keeps returning to that moment this morning. The eyes that tracked me as I passed. The unshakable feeling that something's different today.

Sean cuts through my worry, looking back and forth at me and Pinal. "Anyone wanna know what I've been working on since my promotion?"

Pinal and I stop eating.

"I'm creating an app that will be implanted into cyborgs. The app can translate every language within seconds." Sean snaps his fingers for emphasis. "Milliseconds."

Pinal sits forward, intrigued. "That's fucking cool. So, in a sense, we'll all be speaking one language, and we can all communicate with each other?"

Sean nods, and as if to elaborate, he says, "Exactemento. Exactement. Exactly."

I lift my hand, like we're in class. Sean turns to me. "Can humans use it?"

Sean frowns. "We don't interact with humans, so it doesn't matter."

*

Later, after work, Sean and I walk part of the way home together, to the fork at the end of the street. He turns left, I turn right. This evening, the city is blanketed in white. It's cold. I want to ask a cyborg a question about humans, but I don't know anyone well enough. Except maybe Sean and Pinal. So I ask. "Ever been curious what it would be like to co-exist with humans?"

I've been to Sean's apartment a few years back. His apartment is on the edge of Cyborg City, bordering the human neighborhood, separated only by a thick concrete wall. On the other side, life rages in a way that feels like chaos. There are the drunks, the crippling poverty, the desperate laughter. The kind of laughter that grates on you, sharp and unrestrained. It's the noise of derelicts and lost souls who live outside the borders of our perfect society. Their existence is raw and untamed, and it drives Sean crazy.

The noise invades his space, slipping through cracks in the walls, no matter how thick the concrete is. When the humans are out there, carrying on in their own disordered way, they seep through everything.

Sean tells me, every time, bitterness lacing his voice that he has opened his window and shouted out at them to leave, to stop disturbing his perfect existence. But his words always fall on deaf ears. He says they just laugh at him—loud, uncaring—as if his words have no weight. His frustration boils over, but it's never enough to break the cycle. The humans brush him off, their drunken voices a reminder of the freedom they have to exist, however imperfectly.

Sometimes, after he shouts, they do leave. At least for a while. Then the streets go quiet again. For a few hours, Sean can sleep. But it never lasts. Because the next night, or the night after, the "human trash," as Sean calls them, is back again. They stumble through the streets, their laughter a reminder of everything we've been conditioned to avoid. The chaos, the mess, the rawness of being human.

So Sean's response is not a surprise when I ask if he's curious what it would be like to co-exist with humans.

"Nope."

"Not at all? Never entertained the thought?"

Sean shakes his head emphatically. We walk in silence for a second. I turn to him. And then quietly ask, "Why not?"

"Cuz humans are stupid. Ever seen their social media videos?" Sean scowls. "Look, erase that kind of thinking from your mind. Otherwise, they'll update you. Erase it for you."

I contemplate this in silence for a few seconds. Then I say, almost fearfully, "You're right."

*

Tonight, I'll be going out with Pinal. But I have a few hours to eat and watch documentaries on how humans carried out executions.

I learn human executions were public until about 1939 in Europe and that there were 198 individuals decapitated in Saudi Arabia in 2024. We, cyborgs, claim to be a more developed species, but our recycling and execution "events"—as Pinal calls them—aren't so different.

I learn that public executions were always a spectacle with humans. A brutal, raw exhibition of power that stretches back centuries. In medieval times, executions were as much about maintaining order as they were about spectacle. Crowds gathered in the town squares, eager to witness the punishment of those who had broken the laws of the land. The act itself, whether it was a beheading or a hanging, wasn't just a means of justice. It was meant to show the people the consequences of defiance, to remind them that the power of the monarchy or the state was absolute. The blood, the violence, the drama were all part of the performance, and they served to solidify the grip of those in power. People would watch in awe, some cheering, others recoiling in fear. But it kept the masses in check, rooted in their place. The crowd had to witness, had to feel the terror of what could happen to them.

The execution itself evolved, but the function remained the same. In Saudi Arabia, public executions were still carried out in the open, in dry desert air—the condemned person kneeling before an executioner, often in the presence of a crowd. The law was brutal, and the public nature of it all served as a reminder that the state would not tolerate rebellion, would not tolerate disobedience.

The Western world, too, had its history of public executions, though it largely moved behind closed doors in later years. In the early days of the United States, executions were often held in public, just as they had been in medieval Europe. People would gather, sometimes in the hundreds, to watch as justice was carried out. The hangman's noose, the guillotine, the firing squad, all became symbols not just of justice, but of the public's role in maintaining order. Over time, executions became more private, more clinical, but the idea behind them didn't change. Their goal was to serve as a deterrent, a warning to others who might think of breaking the law.

In our "perfect world", the underlying message is the same: punishment is for public consumption, and your life is worth only as much as your adherence to the rules.

My phone beeps. Pinal's text: "Are you still coming tonight?"

I hesitate, tempted to change my mind. But I text back, reluctantly, "Yes."

CHAPTER 6

We hear the voice before we arrive. "All cyborgs 90 and over will be recycled to keep our population at manageable levels. Cyborgs who are younger can volunteer to be recycled earlier." The voice comes from a large, overhead TV screen, projecting across the large, sterile property.

Although we enter through the main gates, I can see the side entrance where a line of cyborgs in wheelchairs are pushed by nurses to the recycling stage. Each cyborg will be pushed to the center of the stage.

Pinal and I take our seats. Pinal hasn't said much, but I can see his eyes are alive, glowing even. He doesn't want to talk because he thinks it will ruin my expectations. But I can tell he wants to say something. He keeps turning to me, opening his mouth, then closing it.

As we sit and wait, the voice starts up again: "All cyborgs 90 and over will be recycled to keep our population at manageable levels. Cyborgs who are younger can volunteer to be recycled earlier…"

I have not heard of anyone volunteering themselves to be recycled, but Pinal says he knows a couple of male cyborgs who turned themselves in much earlier: one at 53 and the other at 45. They didn't say much, only that they found their day-to-day life too mundane, too boring, and getting up daily had become a chore.

When Pinal tells me this, I want to say that I understand and that I have considered doing the same thing. But I don't want to have Pinal dissecting my life, so I say nothing.

When a nurse wheels an older cyborg to the center of the stage, we all applaud instantaneously. There are whistles and cheers. I peek at Pinal to see his eyes. They look like two flickering balls of fire.

I watch as the nurse tilts the wheelchair forward and waits as the cyborg's body slides into the jaws of a machine.

There's a loud crunching sound. It sounds like a car being crushed. The audience claps and cheers wildly.

I stare in horror. Watching a cyborg getting crushed is disturbing. I turn my head away as the cleaner comes on stage to clean up. The smell is the worst: a combination of metal and blood. It makes me nauseous.

*

Pinal and I walk home. It's late, but I'm not worried. Our society isn't dangerous. There's no crime, and there's no fear of a strange cyborg kidnapping or assaulting me. Violence has been systematically eliminated from our DNA, overwritten like a patch on outdated software. We are always safe. That is, as long as you don't count the cyborg police—watchful and unyielding in their duty to maintain order.

As we step over mounds of snow, Pinal asks what I thought.

"It was interesting."

"That's it? Interesting. It's ingenious. Best way to carry out population control. We don't do that, we all perish. Now, can we do that in the human neighborhoods? Instead of letting them just breed like rabbits?"

It's a good point, but I'm still torn. I like humans: their passion, their fiery personalities, their *range* of personalities. All I can muster up is, "They breed like rabbits but they had some great artists."

Pinal waves his hand, dismissive. "Art can be computer-generated. Need something to hang on your wall? Put an algorithm into a software. Need some music? Get it computer-generated. It's easy."

I try to jump in to say that AI art doesn't have "personality," but Pinal cuts me off. "But engineers? Like me? Society needs more of. Minds that can update our software to generate a more perfect society? Iron out all the kinks? That's what we need. That's genius. Engineering is our future."

"And you're a genius?"

A sneaky smile spreads across Pinal's face. "Just about."

We're outside of Pinal's apartment building now, a stark, boxy structure that blends into the sterile cityscape. He turns to me, his demeanor softening just a little. "This is me. See you tomorrow."

I watch Pinal go inside, thinking he's more human than he'd like to think. Arrogance. That's his human trait. Somewhere in the distance, I hear the faint sound of machinery ... the pulse of our society striving for perfection but always missing the mark.

When Pinal disappears inside his building, I turn around and walk home.

CHAPTER 7

The sound of the neighbor, Don, having sex wakes me up. The woman he's with—a human woman, I'm assuming—is loud. Her cries echo through the paper-thin walls, a stark contrast to the silence that defines our mornings. She climaxes.

Sex is forbidden, but Don knows this already. Everyone knows. It's one of the rules drilled into us from the moment we're created: no physical intimacy. The reasoning, they say, is to maintain order, efficiency, and focus. But rules are rules, and breaking them means consequences: execution or memory upgrades that erase who you are. I imagine Don weighed the risk and decided it was worth it. Maybe he even wanted to be caught. Maybe this was his way of sticking his middle finger up at the sterile, joyless world we live in.

Citizens are expected to report this kind of activity, and there's no shortage of people who would do so willingly, eager for the sense of moral superiority or a small reward. But I won't. It makes me happy that Don has found a sliver of rebellion, a moment of pleasure in our mundane, regulated lives. It's an act of defiance, a reminder that not everyone has been fully beaten into submission.

*

Being woken up to the sounds of sex has changed my attention span. I notice male cyborgs as they walk by. No one is supposed to let their eyes linger as it's perceived as a sexual advance. But today, my eyes want more.

Most of them react the way I expect. They avert their eyes, their programming kicking in, making them dismiss me as irrelevant. But then there's *him*. A male cyborg with light brown hair. He doesn't look away. His eyes, tender and watchful, meet mine. It's not an accident. It's deliberate. The moment stretches beyond what's comfortable, turning into something that feels almost... human. For a few seconds, the world around us fades. There's no sound of footsteps, no distant voices, just this quiet, intimate connection. Then, just as suddenly, I drop my gaze and move on.

*

At my desk, the distraction follows me. His stare lingers in my mind like an echo I can't quite shake. My thoughts keep circling back to it, playing the moment over and over. It wasn't just his stare, though. It was the way it made me feel. Disoriented, unsteady, like I was standing at the edge of something unfamiliar and dangerous. I try to focus on my work, on the blank screen in front of me, but it's no use. The memory of his gaze is burned into my thoughts, a stubborn glitch I can't debug.

*

Maybe it's that male cyborg's stare today, or maybe it's the restlessness that's been simmering under the surface for months, but tonight, I'm feeling adventurous. I need something to break the monotony, something to remind me that life doesn't have to be so sterile. In the human neighborhoods, I've heard, people seeking action or company go to bars for a "drink." Alcohol is forbidden in Cyborg City, of course, as are bars themselves. Vices like that, we're told, are for the weak, distractions from duty. Yet I've also heard whispers of cyborgs sneaking into these places, crossing into human territory to taste the forbidden.

Tonight, it's my turn.

I don't plan it. I just find myself walking, moving past the boundary lines and into a world that feels both foreign and tantalizing. I will learn later, painfully, that I am being watched, that there are cameras on every corner, even in the human neighborhoods. Surveillance doesn't stop at the borders. It never does.

But tonight, I'm blissfully ignorant. I feel sure of myself, bold even. There's a thrill in the act of stepping out of bounds, of choosing something purely for myself.

A red neon sign blinks up ahead, cutting through the fog of the evening. A bar. The air around it feels different. Heavier, warmer, full of sound and smells I don't recognize. I pause as I near the door. I've made it this far, but something about the threshold feels insurmountable. I take a deep breath and count to three, as if the numbers might carry me over. One. Two. Three. Then I push the door open and step inside.

The noise cuts off. The bar goes silent. Every human in the room turns to look at me, their eyes filled with something between curiosity and unease. I don't belong here, and they know it. My presence is an intrusion, a disruption to their world. For a second, the urge to run overwhelms me. I want to turn around, push the door back open, and disappear into the night. But I don't. Somehow, I steady my nerves and force my feet forward, past the wooden tables and the rows of staring eyes, toward the bar.

The bartender is an older man with white, spiky hair. His face is lined with age, but his frame is still strong. His sharp eyes scan me with an intensity that feels both assessing and amused. He doesn't say a word as I approach. I realize I have no idea what to order or how this works. I'm out of my depth, but there's no turning back now. I sit down on the stool in front of him.

I'm unsure what to say, what to ask for. "Can I order alcohol?"

He stifles a laugh. "What do you want?"

I don't know what to order. I take the room in: it's dark, dirty, old. I see glasses with different kinds of liquid in them, some clear, some brown. I look back at the bartender, stumped.

There's a slight smile on the corner of his lips. "We got beer, vodka, whiskey, cocktails."

I don't know what any of these drinks mean. I look over at a poster hanging on the wall behind the bar. It's a beautiful, glamorous human woman with a drink in front of her. I point to the poster. "What's that drink?"

The bartender follows my gaze. "Martini."

"I'll have a martini please."

The bartender nods, starts making my drink, so it

looks just like the poster. He passes me the glass. I'm scared to sip. For a minute, I just stare at it. Then I look up at him. "Let me ask you something."

"Go ahead."

I lean forward so no-one around me can listen in. "What was it like before? Before us?"

The bartender stops cleaning glasses, looks at me for what seems like the first time. "I was still here. Tending bar. Been here for years. So, not much has changed for me."

"What about the neighborhood around you?" I take a sip of my martini while he contemplates the question. The drink is bitter, but I force myself to swallow. I don't get the appeal.

"When things changed, I was young. Stupid. Made some stupid mistakes. I'm older now. Wiser." He shrugs. "So, for me, these days are the better days, you know? I get up and make better decisions. I'm not just throwin' my life away."

I nod, try a different direction. "But is society better with humans in charge? Or better with cyborgs in charge?"

"Like I said, I've been here every day for over fifty years. My life just hasn't changed much either way."

I suddenly realize it's pointless to keep asking. Instead, I take a few more sips of my martini. I half-turn towards the room, watching how humans interact with each other. I motion to the women and ask the bartender, "What are they drinking?"

The bartender follows my finger. "Beer. We got lots of that."

"Maybe I'll try that next time."

The bartender smiles.

*

An hour later, the streets feel emptier, and the human neighborhood feels more menacing and dangerous. Down one of the alleys, there's noise, shouts, arguing.

A cyborg's police car's flashing lights cut across the faces of the human crowd. A cyborg in uniform is out of his car, shoving the crowd back. I move forward, curious to see what all the commotion is. I've only seen "violence" on TV and in documentaries.

A cyborg cop notices me. "Excuse me."

I want to turn around, but he's approaching me now.

He stops a foot away from me. "What are you doing in this neighborhood? It's late. It's dangerous."

Human eyes shift to me. "I was taking a walk. I must have wandered too far."

"Alright, get out of here."

I turn and walk away quickly, knowing his eyes are watching me, suspiciously. What I am not aware of, but will learn later, is that when I enter my apartment building, there's a cyborg in a car, watching me. And his job is to record my every movement from here on.

CHAPTER 8

At lunch, Sean is animated. He made a "no trespassing sign" on his computer that said,

NO TRESPASSING: THIS PROPERTY IS
PROTECTED BY VIDEO
SURVEILLANCE. TRESPASSERS WILL BE
PROSECUTED

Then he printed the sign on metal and hammered it into the fence, right below his apartment, in the human neighborhood. For the past week, he watched through a slit in his blinds to see if "human trash" still gathered there. Most humans thought the sign was real and moved on.

Pinal is amused. "So, you just took that shit from your computer, had it printed on metal, and stuck it on a fence?"

"Hell yeah."

Pinal lets out a loud guffaw.

Sean is smiling now. "That's right. Now they move on, move somewhere else." And under his breath he adds, "Human pieces of shit."

Pinal and I take this moment in. Then Pinal changes the subject abruptly. "You know," he says, looking straight at me. "You're being a patriotic citizen when you watch an execution. Every citizen should watch at least one execution in their lifetime. It's their duty."

Sean and I exchange a glance. Pinal waits

expectantly. I don't like the sudden turn in conversation, but I nod reluctantly.

*

On the way home, I wait at the elevator. The doors slide open, and there he is. HIM. The male cyborg. The one who held my stare the other day. My breath catches for a moment, and my nerves come alive, buzzing under my skin like static. I step into the elevator, pretending not to notice him, but my movements feel stiff, calculated. It's just the two of us now. The small space feels too confined, the air heavy with something I can't name. Should I say something? Would it even matter if I did?

Instead, I turn and press the button for the lobby floor, my finger lingering on the cool surface for a moment too long. The door closes, sealing us in. The descent begins, smooth and soundless, but each passing second feels stretched, as if time itself has slowed. I keep my gaze fixed on the numbers above the door, watching them tick downward, willing them to move faster. My heart, however, has its own rhythm. Quick, erratic.

I can feel him, his presence filling the space even though he hasn't moved or spoken. Should I turn to him? Acknowledge him? Say something, anything? But I don't. My courage falters, and the silence between us grows louder. I wonder if he's watching me, if he's as aware of this strange, charged moment as I am. And then I know. I *feel* his eyes on me, their weight pressing into my back, tracing the lines of my silhouette. It's subtle, but it's there, unmistakable.

When the elevator finally dings and the doors slide open, I step out quickly, eager to escape the tension, yet reluctant to leave it behind. As I walk into the writing offices, I can sense him still watching me, his gaze following me even as the space between us widens. A small part of me screams to turn back, to say something, to bridge this unspoken connection before it fades into nothingness. But my feet keep moving, and my mouth stays closed. The moment slips away, unspoken words hanging in the air like ghosts.

By the time I reach my desk, I glance back over my shoulder, half-hoping to catch another glimpse of him, to find him still standing there in the elevator. But the doors are already closed, and he's gone.

CHAPTER 9

I've never seen an execution, but I've seen the reality TV show, *The Executioner's Diaries*. It's about Craig, the executioner, and his life. Every show starts the same way: Craig lies on his back in a dark room, staring up at the ceiling. He gets up slowly, walks over to a digital calendar on the wall, where there are big, red Xs. With his finger, he draws another large X. The next box says, "EXECUTION DAY."

The following scene, Craig sips black coffee, looks out of the cloudy window towards the street. And then we cut to a live, televised execution.

I always turn the TV off at this point, and I do today as well. My phone beeps. It's Pinal. "You're still coming?"

I think about my answer for almost a minute. Finally, I type in. "Sure."

*

Later that evening, Pinal and I, alongside other Cyborgs, walk single file into a room. Inside a dark auditorium, we all take a seat, facing a glass divider. There's a buzz in the room, uncontained excitement, like the anticipation in a room right before a circus act. All eyes stay riveted on the glass divider and the hallway behind it.

Behind the glass wall, a cyborg is led in, blindfolded. Craig, the executioner—now hooded—follows. We watch in silence as Craig and the cyborg take their places 10 feet apart. A bell sounds.

Craig lifts a gun and points it at the back of the Cyborg's head.

Another bell sounds. And as it does, I catch my breath. The gun goes off, and the bullet hits the cyborg in the back of the head, sending him to the floor. He collapses on the floor with a thud, limbs flapping wildly like a puppet. Then he becomes lifeless.

The scene scares me, but I notice Pinal's eyes shining with a strange sort of glee.

*

That night, I relive every moment, unable to sleep. The image keeps replaying: the executioner shooting and the cyborg going down. Even when I close my eyes, the image is there, beneath my eyelids.

*

The next day, at my desk, I'm distracted. The air feels thick, as if the world itself is pressing down on me, suffocating me with its weight. Every sound seems too loud, every movement too sudden, and the office sounds only amplify the noises in my head. There are things I wish I hadn't seen, moments I can't unsee, and now, those images linger in my mind—the execution, the cyborg going down, the strange applause like a crowd cheering a circus performance.

I stand up finally, needing space, needing air. My feet move on their own as I wander the hallways, the sterile white walls offering no comfort, the harsh lighting casting everything in a clinical, dispassionate glow. I don't have a clear direction. I'm just moving, letting my thoughts spiral. My mind refuses to settle, the dissonance of yesterday's execution still playing in the back of my mind.

Then, in the hallway, a solitary figure moves toward me. At first, he's just a shadow in the distance, indistinct, blurred like a mirage. But slowly, as if pulled into sharper focus by some unseen force, he becomes clearer. I notice the shape, the posture, the familiar stride. It's HIM. My breath catches in my chest. My knees buckle just a little. He's here, walking toward me, his focus set firmly on me.

He's so close now, and yet still far enough to keep the tension building, the unspoken weight of his gaze pressing into me like a tangible force. His eyes meet mine, and for a second, time slows. Every dark moment, every troubling thought that had been clouding my mind vanishes in an instant. It's just the two of us, and the noise of the world fades away.

As he nears, my body reacts on instinct. I step to the side, my movements stiff, trying to make space, trying to maintain some semblance of control. But he doesn't change his course. He's still coming toward me, walking fast. There's no hesitation in his steps, no sign of slowing down.

And then, just as the air feels like it might snap, he collides with me. It's not harsh or forceful, but it's enough to make my breath hitch, enough to send a shiver through me. His voice cuts through the brief silence that follows, soft and apologetic. "I'm sorry," he says, his eyes widening in surprise, then softening as if he hadn't meant for this to happen.

There's something in his voice, an undercurrent of sincerity, maybe even uncertainty. I want to speak, to brush off the awkwardness, but the words get caught in my throat.

Before I can respond or pull away, he slips something into my hand. It's quick, almost too quick to process, and before I can register what's happened, I'm left standing there, staring at the piece of paper he's just placed in my palm. My fingers tremble as I grasp it, my heart racing. I'm so nervous that I almost drop it. It's absurd, but it feels like the most important thing in the world right now.

I'm unsure of what to do next. My instinct is to go to my desk, to read it there in the safety of my routine, but something tells me that's too dangerous. I need more privacy. I need to be somewhere where no one can see me, where I can process whatever this is. My eyes move toward the restroom, and without thinking, I hurry in that direction.

The door clicks shut behind me, and I lean against it for a moment, trying to calm my nerves, my thoughts. My hands shake as I unfold the paper, the crisp sound of the edges crackling in the silence of the restroom. I sit down on the toilet, eyes fixed on the words, the moment feeling surreal, as if I've crossed some invisible threshold into a world I can't quite understand.

I read the note three times, each pass a slow

unraveling of my thoughts, trying to piece together the meaning. My mind races, but it's not until the fourth reading that the message finally sinks in. It's simple, direct, and yet the weight of it is overwhelming.

CAN WE MEET?

HUMANITY

CHAPTER 10

I'm torn. I don't know what to do. To meet or not to meet. I think about him all the time, every day, every minute. Sometimes, I'm sure I know what to do. Other times, I'm back to square one. Undecided.

There are times I see him in the cafeteria or in the hallway, but I turn away, keep my head down, afraid of what will happen if we meet eyes. Yet, I *want* to meet eyes. I want this relationship. And yet...

I'm with Sean and Pinal in the cafeteria, but my thoughts are on HIM. I know Sean is saying something, but it doesn't register. It's noise on the periphery of my brain.

"They got eliminated. Shot."

Pinal nods. "Why?"

"Indulging in human behavior. Watching porn. Having passionate relationships."

Sean's last sentence gets my attention. "What'd you say?"

"I said I heard a couple of cyborgs got eliminated for having passionate relationships."

"Eliminated how?"

"Shot. Back of the head."

Pinal is nodding. "Yep. Executed."

Sean is nodding, too. "Then their metal gets recycled and their flesh gets cremated."

This gruesome image silences me.

*

The top TV show right now is *The Executioner's Diary*, where we, the audience, get to be voyeurs in the life of the male cyborg who decides fates with a trigger pull. Every week, we watch as he scratches off a red X on his calendar, marking "execution day." The ritual is always the same: a deep breath, a moment of stillness, the red marker moving across the screen.

Like the rest of the city, I'm fascinated with his misery. His internal war. His slow unraveling. His "reality show" is morbid, like watching an accident on the road. Gruesome and haunting. The show cuts between scenes of him standing in front of a mirror, staring into his own eyes, and flashes of his hands—steady, practiced, deadly—holding the gun.

In the final minutes of each episode, the execution happens. It's never shown directly, just the sound of the shot, the abrupt cut to black. The silence that follows is deafening. And then, as if nothing happened, the credits roll.

*

I don't know why I keep returning to the human neighborhood. Maybe it's to take my mind off HIM. Maybe it's to find the mother in my dreams. Or maybe it's just to escape my world.

Today, I walk down an alley, the air thick with the scent of damp pavement and old cooking grease. A neon sign flickers above a rusted doorway, casting jagged shadows against the walls. That's when I see him: a homeless man perched on the corner, muttering to himself, rocking slightly on his heels.

He keeps repeating the same phrases over and over again, with the same passion. "That's what I said! You think I don't know that? I been saying that from the beginning!" His voice is raw, stretched thin like a rope about to snap.

A few steps forward, and he repeats it again. "That's what I said! You think I don't know that? I been saying that from the beginning!"

His frenzied repetitions unsettle me, like an incantation winding itself around my bones. I try to walk past him, to become invisible, but my eyes betray me. They meet his for a fraction of a second. Too long. His gaze latches onto mine like a hook, and his expression shifts, something sparking in the unsettled corners of his mind.

I drop my eyes quickly, but it's too late. The eye contact is an acknowledgment, an invitation. He rises, his tattered coat flaring slightly as he takes his first step toward me.

I keep walking. Faster now. But I can hear him behind me, the uneven shuffle of his footsteps, closing the distance. I can feel his breath on the back of my neck, or maybe it's just my fear making me hypersensitive. My pulse quickens.

I scan the street. There's an antique store to my left, its window cluttered with tarnished silverware. I almost rip the door open in my desperation to escape. The bell above the door jingles violently as I step inside.

The scent of aged paper and furniture polish rushes over me. I turn to the window, heart pounding, watching for his silhouette.

He pauses outside. Stares darkly at me. For a second, I think he might enter. But something changes in him, some private logic, some unseen force pulling him elsewhere. He mutters something under his breath and turns, disappearing back into the street, his presence evaporating like mist.

I exhale, long and slow.

*

Now that I'm in the store, I'm curious. I've never been in an "antique" store before. I don't know what I expected, but it's shabbier than I imagined. I can smell dust, varnish, and something older, like time itself has settled into the cracks of the wooden floor.

Antiques are everywhere, cluttered on shelves, piled into corners, leaning against walls. A ceiling fan creaks above, pushing warm, stale air in slow, lazy circles.

The owner of the store is at a desk, an old overweight woman. Long white hair and droopy eyelids. She's hunched over, scrutinizing an old clock. She finally looks up. "Hello. Welcome."

I smile back and then let my gaze shift to the items displayed: old furniture, clocks, watches in glass cases, TVs. Then I stop at something different: pottery. Dozens of designs, each unique, some smooth and glossy, others rough and cracked, their colors swirled like they captured emotion itself in clay. They don't look manufactured, like the precise, sterile creations of machines. These have… imperfections.

The owner joins me, moving slowly, her cane tapping against the floor. She leans in slightly, her voice quieter now, like she's sharing a secret. "Those are from our local artists. We have a pottery class weekly in the back. These are some of their creations."

"They created these themselves? They're not computer-generated?"

The owner laughs, a brief, sharp cackle. "Yes. Created them in our weekly pottery class. They're nice, aren't they?"

I'm mesmerized. "They're created with… passion."

"I guess you could say that."

I lift one up. It's small. A deep blue bowl with uneven edges, as if the creator's hands trembled while shaping it. My fingers run over the surface, feeling the slight ridges, the human touch.

"I'll buy this one."

The owner smiles, her eye wrinkles deepening. "Good. I'll wrap it up for you."

*

At home, I carefully take my pottery out of its bag and place it on my table. It's my souvenir from the human neighborhood. The deep blue glaze catches the light, shifting in shades, almost like it's breathing. I stare at it for a minute, content.

This discovery leads me back the next day. I still don't know what I'm looking for.

I open up the antique store, excited. The door

sticks at first, then jerks open. The owner is at her desk, hunched over the same clock. "You again," she says, her voice grainy, like paper rubbing against sandpaper.

"I thought I'd buy something else."

Her lips twitch into the smallest of smiles. "That's a good sign."

I start to browse, moving slower this time. The cluttered shelves feel different today. Less chaotic, more intentional. I breathe in the dust, the polish, the lingering scent of something unidentifiable. Each piece feels like a fragment of something bigger, a puzzle I haven't put together yet.

My feet lead me toward the back of the store. Then I stop.

There are stairs.

I didn't notice them yesterday.

They rise steeply, leading up to a closed door. The wood is old, the paint chipped at the edges. There's a single, yellowed lightbulb above, glowing weakly.

The owner limps toward me, following my gaze. Her cane taps against the wooden floor, the sound steady, deliberate.

"That's a small room. When I first opened the store, my husband and I would stay up there... It was just too busy to go home. But when the store started doing better, we didn't need to stay there anymore..."

I listen, fascinated.

"Anyway, years went by. Sometimes, we'd let students rent it for a semester. But the university closed. Then my husband passed. And now..." Her voice softens. "Now it's just an empty room. It still has a has a little furniture though."

"Can I see it?"

"Sure."

*

We go up the stairs. The floors creak on every step. At the top, we stand side by side as the owner pushes the door aside. I step inside cautiously, look around, feeling the layers of dust go through my nostrils. The scent of age fills the air. Wood, paper, something faintly metallic. The space is small, but it doesn't feel cramped. Just… still.

A single window lets in dim light, casting soft, elongated shadows. The bed against the far wall is narrow, its blanket neatly folded despite the dust settled over it. A wooden shelf stands against another wall, nearly bare except for a few books, their spines cracked, their titles faded.

And then there's the painting.

It hangs slightly crooked on the wall, the colors muted but clear. An empty field stretching into the distance, golden grass swaying under a sky caught between dusk and dawn.

I stare at it. "Is the painting real?" My voice is quieter than I expect. "Or AI?"

The owner laughs quietly. The question amuses her. "Real."

I nod, still taking in the room, letting it settle into me.

It's an unremarkable room. Small, uninteresting.

And yet, I feel something deep in my bones, like I've arrived at a place I didn't know I was searching for.

I don't say anything.

But somehow, I know.

This is what I came for.

CHAPTER 11

Home. I'm exhausted. I should be in bed, not scrolling through the TV shows. But *The Executioner's Diary* catches my eye. It's about recycling and he's talking to a Woebot. I crank up the volume. On the TV screen, Craig, the executioner, stares at an application online. He presses the "Chat" button.

A cyborg's face appears online. "Hello. Are you inquiring about our recycling schedule?"

Yes.

"What can I help you with?"

Craig's face distorts slightly. He measures his words. "I would like to volunteer myself to be recycled."

The cyborg nods, as though it were a daily bank transaction. "Okay. I can get you started on that. May I ask why?"

Craig takes a few seconds to formulate his words. Finally. "I'm an executioner. It's taken its toll."

"I understand. Part of our application process involves mental health counseling with our in-house WoeBot. Can I set up an appointment?"

"Why?"

"We want to make sure that you're making the right decision. Recycling is final. And voluntary recycling is what we call… suicide."

Craig sits up, emphatic. "That's exactly what I want."

"I understand. But, counseling is required with our in-house WoeBot. Can I set up an appointment?"

"This is necessary?"

"It is."

A long beat. Craig looks down. Finally, his gaze lifts and rests on the cyborg. "Okay."

The session ends. The screen fades to black. Craig stares at his reflection in the darkened glass.

*

I turn the TV off, intrigued. Disturbed. I'm sure that one day our paths will cross. How, I'm not sure.

That night, I dream about Craig. We're in the execution room, and his gun is pointed at me. He fires the gun, and I crumple to the floor like a puppet. The sensation is strange. Not pain, but a hollow collapse, like I was never solid to begin with. Craig looks down at me, his expression unreadable. I wake up gasping.

When I wake up, I know my decision. I will meet with HIM. I walk to work with a purpose. The cyborg police are arresting two cyborgs—for what I'm not sure. That should deter me, give me pause. But I soldier on. The air feels heavier today, charged with something unsaid. I catch snippets of hushed conversations, nervous glances exchanged between colleagues. There's a tension pressing against the walls, against my skin. But I don't stop.

*

In the hallway, I see HIM. I know he goes to the bathroom at the exact same time every day, and so I coincide my bathroom break with his.

We walk towards each other. I'm nervous. It's the right decision, but I keep thinking... maybe it's too late, maybe he's changed his mind. Maybe his desire has waned.

But there he is. When we pass, I slip the piece of paper into his hand. It says simply, "WHERE?"

I walk to my desk and breathe.

*

The rest of the day passes in a blur. Conversations drift past me, unregistered. The city outside seems sharper, somehow. The edges of buildings too defined, the neon signs too bright. I check the time repeatedly, watching the hours fold into evening.

By the time I leave work, the streets feel different. Less crowded, more watchful. I keep my head down, my hands in my pockets. Every step takes me closer. Closer to HIM. Closer to whatever comes next.

*

On my way home, I see a prostitute stepping out of my neighbor Don's apartment, adjusting her dress. She keeps her head lowered, avoiding my eyes, before disappearing down the hallway. Don stands in the doorway for a moment, watching her go, then slips back inside. The door clicks shut, sealing away his secret, but I know better. Nothing is truly secret anymore. Not in this city. Not under their watchful eyes.

I envy him. Not just his recklessness, but his

51

certainty. The brazen hunger that drives him to seek out passion despite the risk. The raw, unfiltered indulgence in pleasure, in flesh, in something that feels real in a world where so little does. He has had sex. He has felt desire and let it consume him. And though he knows the consequences, he still reaches for it.

But his days are numbered. The cyborg police know. They *always* know. They are watching, waiting, biding their time. The rules are clear, and Don has broken them. His reckoning will come.

*

I lie in bed, staring at the ceiling, listening to the surveillance drones. The city never sleeps, and neither do they. But I know now, with a certainty that settles deep in my bones, that I have already made my decision. I will walk the same path. I will taste passion, intimacy, sex— though not in the way Don has. My desire has a name. Romance.

And the moment we meet, I know my days will be numbered, just like Don's. And nothing will ever be the same.

CHAPTER 12

The answer comes the next day.

I'm in the hallway again, at the exact same time. HE is there, at the exact same time. It isn't coincidence. It isn't fate. It's intention, calculation, a step forward in a dance neither of us can afford to misstep.

He will slip me a piece of paper. He will tell me where.

We walk toward each other, the distance between us shrinking with every step. My heart is hammering, the sound filling my ears until it drowns out everything else. My vision tunnels, blurs, then snaps into focus again. My senses feel like they're betraying me, slipping from my grasp. The air is thick, charged, electric. My palms are slick with sweat, too damp to hold onto anything.

And then ... contact.

The moment his fingers brush mine, a shock runs up my arm, an absurd, impossible thrill. The paper is pressed into my palm, smooth and small, and then he is gone, passing me as if nothing happened. As if we are nothing to each other.

I don't stop walking. I move forward, feigning boredom, nonchalance. Until I reach the bathroom. The door closes behind me with a hollow click, sealing me away from the rest of the world. My breath is ragged. My fingers tremble as I unfold the slip of paper, nearly tearing it in my urgency.

The words stare back at me, black ink on white:

Barton Creek Square. Saturday. 1 p.m.

I read it once. Twice. Over and over again until the letters blur. My chest tightens, my breath coming fast, too fast. Am I hyperventilating? It feels like I am.

Excitement. Fear.

I will be there.

No matter what it takes, I will be there.

*

I'm at Barton Creek Square fifteen minutes early. There's a rally and a speaker, and the square is crowded. I'm not sure how the male cyborg will find me. I stand back, scanning the faces, looking for him. The crowd applauds.

I walk up and down the square, waiting for time to pass. The crowd thickens. I check my watch again. 12:57 pm. I stand by a streetlight, a little removed from the crowd. I'm nervous now, thinking he won't show. Or maybe he changed his mind. I think up all types of scenarios on why he chose not to come. I'm also not sure why he chose a crowded place—everyone can see us.

Then from the distance, I see him coming. I exhale nervously, trying to calm myself. He motions me to move towards the crowd, and I obey. Now he's next to me, but we're both facing the speaker. He speaks, his voice low and steady, but he never looks at me.

"I'm Neal."

I turn to look at his profile, but he stares ahead. His features are sharper than I expected, angular.

"And you are?"

"I'm Cynthia."

Then Neal turns to me. We look into each other's eyes. The world seems to slow. There's an intensity in his gaze, something calculating yet not unkind. For a moment, I feel stripped bare. "Can you meet on Sunday?"

"Yes."

"Reflection Lake. Do you know it?"

I shake my head. I've never heard of such a place.

"Look it up on your phone. When you get there, follow the signs to the water. Once you see the water, walk for half a mile. There's a bench. I'll be there." His voice is calm, directive. Not a request, but a statement of fact. My fingers itch to reach for my phone, to confirm the place exists, but I resist. Instead, I nod, swallowing.

He looks at me again, and my heart flutters. "Think you can remember that?"

I nod. "What time?"

"One pm."

I nod again. A chant rises from the crowd, swelling around us. It feels like a wave, the kind that could pull you under if you're not careful. The moment between us shatters as reality presses back in.

"See you then."

Neal abruptly turns away from me and walks in the direction he came. His departure is as precise as his arrival. No hesitation, no second glance.

I watch him until the sea of people swallows him whole. The chant continues, voices rising in unison, but I barely hear it. My thoughts are elsewhere, tangled in the uncertainty of what comes next.

Reflection Lake.

One pm.

A bench.

CHAPTER 13

The flickering TV screen washes my living room in shifting colors. But I can't concentrate. My mind keeps drifting back to Reflection Lake.

There's shouting in the hallway.

I stand, hurry towards the door. A neighbor cyborg—bitter, eyes squinting in fury—is shouting at Don, who has just arrived with groceries. I catch the last of her rant, looking through my door's peephole.

"You won't get away with it. I see that human coming in and out. I'll report you, you know."

She slams her door hard.

Don doesn't move at first. Then, like something inside him breaks, he drops the groceries. He sinks down to the floor, his hands covering his face, his shoulders trembling with quiet sobs.

I watch him cry silently. My hand goes to the doorknob, but I stop myself. If I get involved, if I console him, she'll report me too.

The walls feel thinner than they are. Don shakes with grief, alone. I step backward, my body consumed with a silent ache. The TV still plays in the background, voices and laughter from some scripted reality far removed from this one. I sit back down, staring at the screen without seeing it.

In the hallway, Don's sobs fade.

*

My first thought about Reflection Lake is that it's

stunning. The name fits perfectly. Its still surface mirrors the sky so flawlessly that it's hard to tell where the water ends and the air begins. Clouds drift lazily across both the sky and its twin below, their edges tinged with the soft gold of the setting sun. A perfect, endless reflection.

My second thought is that Neal won't be there.

But then I see him. He's sitting on a black, metal bench near the water's edge. The glow of the fading sun casts a long shadow behind him. Even his calm, composed silhouette makes my heart stop.

I hesitate for a moment before walking over, every step making me more aware of the quiet that surrounds us. The only sounds are the gentle lapping of water against the shore. When I reach him, I sit down, careful to leave just enough space between us. Close enough to feel his presence, far enough that it doesn't feel too bold.

For a long moment, we just sit there. Neither of us speaks. The silence isn't heavy, exactly, but it's charged with something unspoken. A tension that feels like the edge of a new beginning. Then, finally, I ask, "Why me?"

Neal turns his head slightly, studying me with those unreadable eyes of his. "I saw something in your eyes. A little more... humanity than the others."

I swallow, my gaze shifting back to the lake. The water ripples slightly, distorting the reflection of the sky. His words sit with me, settling somewhere deep.

The silence stretches again, but this time, it's different. Not empty, just unhurried. Like he's perfectly fine sitting here forever without another word.

I glance at him. His profile is serene, but there's

a quiet intensity beneath it, something thoughtful.

"What now?" I ask.

"I don't know," he admits. "Get to know each other. Become friends. Maybe more."

Our eyes meet then. His are steady, magnetic, pulling me in with a quiet certainty. I feel the moment change, something new unfolding between us.

"Maybe more." That's what makes my heart flutter.

CHAPTER 14

A week after meeting Neal, I meet Eddie. Eddie is human and a photographer. He tells me this almost immediately. He takes portraits because he enjoys capturing moments, personalities, a little bit of peoples' souls that might otherwise disappear. It's a very human thing to say.

His voice is sharp, but there's no fear in it. Just curiosity. Bold. Direct. Most humans aren't brave enough to talk to a cyborg, especially not like this. That alone fascinates me. I like him immediately.

I stop, quietly studying him. His face is lined, not with age, but with experience. His eyes hold something weary but alive, like he's always listening, always taking you in.

"I'm meeting someone," I say.

"A human?"

A beat. I consider my answer, but then decide he won't care. "A cyborg."

Eddie lets out a short breath, surprised. He steps away from his makeshift fire and falls into step beside me as I start walking again. "Why here?" he asks. "Why this neighborhood?"

"I like it better."

He glances at me, curiously, like he wants to ask something but changes his mind.

"I'm Cynthia. Thirty 84," I say. What's your name?"

"Eddie Rouse," he says. "We don't get numbers. We get last names."

I nod. "I like that. Makes you unique."

Eddie smiles, just for a second, before his gaze drifts back to the street. The buildings sag under years of neglect. Potholes big enough to swallow a bicycle litter the road. The neon signs above the few open businesses flicker unevenly.

"Your neighborhood has grit. Personality," I say, taking it all in.

Eddie laughs, but there's no humor in it. "All I see are a bunch of losers, just going down."

I shake my head. I want to argue, to tell him that decay isn't the same as defeat, that a place can be broken and still have a soul. But before I can say anything, Eddie keeps talking.

"You know," he says, his voice quieter now, more thoughtful, "I heard somewhere… in another country, they let people like me and people… cyborgs… like you sit side by side. We're even in government together. Making laws together."

I stop walking. "Where?"

He shrugs. "I don't know. Just heard it was some other place."

"Where'd you hear it from?"

Eddie hesitates. His gaze flickers away, scanning the darkened windows above us, the alley behind, as if the answer might be hiding there. "People talk," he says finally.

I think about that. About the possibility of such a place existing. A world where humans and cyborgs aren't separated by fear, law, or hatred. "I wish that were true," I say.

There's a brief flash of anger in Eddie's eyes. "It's true! And it's possible. Equals. A society with both of us side by side."

I hold his gaze, but I don't answer right away. His belief is so strong, so certain, that I almost want to believe it too. But I've seen too much to accept it so easily. "Now that, Eddie," I say quietly, "sounds like utopia."

I keep walking, but Eddie has stopped, bothered.

He doesn't say anything else.

But I can tell he doesn't like my answer.

*

I'm in the small room above the antique store. The owner has kindly let me rent it out, a quiet little hideaway tucked above shelves of forgotten trinkets and old stories. The wooden floors creak softly as I move about, setting things up. A candle flickers on the small table, casting warm shadows along the walls. Two plates, two cups, a modest spread of snacks. Just enough to make it feel intentional. I smooth out the tablecloth, take a step back, and let my eyes drift over the space. It's simple but inviting, the kind of setting that makes you want to linger. A place where words come easier.

A knock at the door.

Neal.

My heart flutters, a nervous little tremor in my chest. I take a slow breath, try to steady myself, but the anticipation is already sweeping through me. Just knowing he's on the other side of that door makes me feel unsteady in a way I haven't felt in a long time.

I cross the room, fingers cool against the brass doorknob. A pause, just a fraction of a second, before I pull it open.

And there he is.

The light from the hallway spills over him, catching the easy tilt of his smile, the familiar way he stands. His eyes meet mine, searching, warm. I step back, a silent invitation.

Neal enters, glancing around with mild curiosity. The candlelight flickers in his eyes, making it hard to read his expression. He says finally, "Except for the crappy neighborhood it's in, this is nice. How'd you find this place?"

"I was shopping downstairs, and I noticed the stairs. The owner agreed to rent it to me."

Neal nods as if that makes sense, then moves toward the bed. He sits, watching me with a look I can't quite decipher. Something suggestive, lingering just at the edge of his smile.

I hesitate before joining him, sitting on the edge, deliberately leaving a wide space between us. The distance is intentional. He notices, of course. His lips twitch, barely holding back his amusement.

The silence stretches too long. I search for something to say, something to cut through the sudden weight in the air. "What's your job?" The words come out quicker than I intend, almost awkward in their abruptness.

Neal watches me for a beat before answering. "I create algorithms in cyborgs... in us... that remove their 'humanity.'" His voice is calm, matter-of-fact. "Right now, we're all a different mix. Some more cyborg than others, some more human than others." He pauses, as if measuring his next words. "The goal is to remove all feelings."

"In order to create a perfect society," I say, more statement than question.

Neal nods. "That's right."

I shift slightly, closing some of the space between us. His eyes shift to mine. We hold the stare, a quiet tension filling the room. My pulse picks up. The candlelight makes everything feel softer, more fragile. I swallow and lower my voice to almost a whisper.

"You know what my previous job was?"

Neal waits.

"I used to work in the porn industry. We created algorithms to weaken our sex drives. We experimented with porn videos and had cyborgs watch them to gauge their reaction. Only female cyborgs worked there. Male cyborgs have less controllable sex instincts than female cyborgs. So, they're in greater danger of being corrupted."

"What happens to the cyborgs that got turned on by watching porn videos?"

"We measured it. If it was a lot, the cyborg got shot... executed."

Neal winces.

I continue. "If it was a small amount, the government would look into deleting just part of the cyborg's drive. Then they would do an update."

*

Hours later, Neal and I are in bed, tangled in the comfortable silence. The world outside feels distant, like a forgotten dream. The candle has burned low, casting long shadows across the room. The air is warm, still carrying the faint scent of wax and something unnameable, something that belongs only to this moment.

We lie facing each other, our bodies close but not quite touching. His breath is steady, his gaze unblinking. I lose myself in the depth of his eyes, dark pools that pull me under, and I think, so this is what cloud nine feels like. Weightless. Timeless. Like nothing outside this room exists.

Neither of us speaks. There's no need. We just breathe each other in, lost in the surrealness of it all. His fingertips trace absent patterns on my skin, and I follow the slow, rhythmic movement, hypnotized. I feel the pull of reality waiting outside, its sharp edges ready to cut through the softness of this moment. But I don't want to go back.

Not yet. Maybe not ever.

*

Returning home that evening, the air feels harsh and cold. There's a brutal wind. When I turn the corner toward my apartment, I see it. The car. Parked just slightly out of place, angled toward the streetlight as if positioned for a better view. My stomach tightens. My breath catches. And then I see him: a male cyborg in the driver's seat. He's a dark silhouette against the streetlight, but I can tell he's watching me.

A shiver crawls up my spine, and for the first time, there is no doubt. No dismissing it as paranoia. No convincing myself it's just a coincidence.

I am being followed.

I am being watched.

The certainty of it settles heavy in my chest. I force myself to keep walking, to pretend I don't see him, don't feel the weight of his gaze. But the air feels thinner now, the night stretched tight with something unseen.

*

At home, I try to steady myself. The warmth of the tea soothes my hands, but not the unease in my stomach. I sit stiffly on the couch, the steam from the cup rising in slow, delicate wisps. The documentary flickers on the screen: a study on human emotions, their passions, the way they speak about love and intimacy as though it's life itself.

I watch, transfixed. I want to understand them. To feel as they do, to brush against the edges of their world with my own emotions. And I do, I *am*. It fills me with a strange exhilaration, a secret thrill that vibrates just beneath my skin. I am not like them, not fully, but I am closer than I have ever been. And I don't want to stop.

Outside, there's noise. Footsteps. Heavy, deliberate. Many of them.

I put my tea down carefully, my breath shallow, my body instinctively still. Then comes the banging.

Loud, relentless, shaking the walls.

I tiptoe to the door, pressing my eye to the peephole.

Ten cyborg police. Armed. They flood into Don's apartment, weapons raised.

I can't move. I can barely breathe.

Seconds later, they drag Don out, his arms wrenched behind his back in tight cuffs. He doesn't struggle. He knows it would be useless. But his face is stamped with something close to fear. Or maybe pain. They shove him forward, his body jolting from the force.

A door opens down the hall. A female cyborg steps out, her expression blank, her gaze locked on Don as they drag him past her. She doesn't speak. She just watches.

No one interferes. No one ever does.

I swallow hard.

This is what sex leads to.

This is what happens when you let yourself feel too much. These are the repercussions for breaking the rules, for stepping too far into what isn't meant to be ours.

I don't know for sure, but deep in my core, I can feel it. I will be next.

CHAPTER 15

Neal and I spend Saturday evening in the human neighborhood, blending into the shadows at the back of the open-air bar. The scent of sweat, beer, and fried food thickens the air. The band on stage plays something lively—electric guitars wailing, drums pulsing—but the music is just a backdrop to the real spectacle: the people.

Most of the wooden tables are full, occupied by groups laughing too loudly, drinking too much. Some people have pushed their chairs back to dance, their bodies moving without inhibition. One woman, in particular, stands out: purple hair, purple shorts, purple sneakers, a purple T-shirt. She's lost in the rhythm, spinning on the worn-down floorboards, her face tilted toward the sky as if this moment belongs only to her.

Nearby, a heavier woman with thick arms and sandaled feet sways to the beat alone, her movements slow but deliberate. She doesn't seem to care who watches.

A man in a hat and glasses stands at the edge of the crowd, tapping one pointed shoe in time with the music. A single feather sticks out from his hat, catching in the dim light as he nods along, absorbed in the melody.

Everywhere, there's beer. Hard liquor. Glass bottles sweating on wooden tables, shot glasses emptied and refilled. Most of the humans here are overweight, their bodies soft, their skin inked with swirling tattoos. Symbols, names, images that mean something only to them. They drink. They laugh. Some of them press close to one another, whispering in each other's ears.

Neal and I remain on the outskirts, away from the heat of the bodies, the thumping bassline vibrating through the floor. We don't dance. We don't drink. We watch.

I lean back into Neal's chest, feeling the solid warmth of him against me. His arms wrap around my waist, his breath hot against my neck as he buries his face there. For a moment, I let myself sink into it, into the quiet illusion of safety.

Then, softly, I turn my face toward him. "They came after my neighbor Don because he was having sex."

"How'd they find out?"

"I don't know," I admit. "I didn't say anything."

I stare ahead at the moving bodies, at the way humans touch each other so freely, so thoughtlessly. They don't realize what it means to have that. What it means to lose it.

"This won't last forever." My voice is barely above a whisper. "You know that, don't you?"

Neal is silent for a long time, watching the band, watching the humans revel in their temporary joy. "I don't care about forever," he finally says. "I care about right now."

*

Later, Neal and I walk through the human neighborhood, the streets alive with conversation, the occasional burst of laughter, the clatter of dishes from unseen kitchens. The air is thick with the mingling scents of human life. Grilled meat, frying oil, something rich and spicy curling through the air from an open window. I breathe it in, savoring the warmth of it, the imperfection, the reality.

Neal walks beside me, his posture stiff, his gaze flicking across the street like he expects danger at every turn. I know this place makes him uncomfortable, that every aspect of human existence—chaotic, unpolished—grates against the very fabric of his being. He despises them, and he has told me so in more ways than one. And yet, he's here. For me.

I glance over at him, at the hard line of his jaw, the way his eyes dart over the crumbling storefronts, the uneven sidewalks, the clusters of humans standing outside small, dimly lit shops. His hand tightens briefly around mine, not out of affection, but out of something closer to obligation. Still, I take it for what it is.

"I love it here," I say, my voice soft but certain. "I love being in the human neighborhood. Nothing like it. The smell of smoke, food in the air. Human faces everywhere. The noise. The chaos.... I'm truly happiest here." I motion toward a corner store where a group of teenagers loiter, laughing too loud, their hands deep in their jacket pockets. "Even the messiness of it. Their imperfections. It would be nice to live here. See this every day."

Neal doesn't respond immediately. He watches me instead. I can tell that he wants to understand, that he wishes he could share my enthusiasm, but there's a wall between us, a fundamental difference in how we see this world.

"I'll take a hard pass on that," he says after a

while.

"I know," I respond quietly.

He exhales, glancing away as if he doesn't want to continue this conversation. I let the silence settle between us, unspoken words hanging in the cool night air. I don't need him to love them the way I do. I just need him to see.

*

When we get to our small room, Neal's body finally relaxes. His shoulders, tense from navigating the human neighborhood, ease as he steps inside. It's only here, away from the noise and unpredictability of the streets, that he lets his guard down. I push open the window, letting in the cool night air.

Down on the sidewalk, two homeless people, a man and a heavy woman, stand beneath a streetlight. A small, battered speaker sits between them, blasting music that crackles with static. They move with the rhythm, lost in their own world. The woman sways her hips, her arms lifting in loose, joyous movements. The man claps his hands, stomps his feet in an uneven beat, grinning as if this moment is all that matters.

I watch them, fascinated. They aren't concerned with where they'll sleep tonight or how they look or who's watching. They are simply here. Alive.

I motion for Neal to join me. When he does, I point to the couple. "She's beautiful."

Neal looks over at her. "She's fat."

"She's human. Imperfect. I like mistakes. I hate

perfection. I hate our perfect world."

Neal watches the couple for a beat longer. Then, with a quiet sigh, he steps away, returning to the bed. He isn't moved. He doesn't see them the way I do.

I take one last look at the pair before closing the window. Then I join Neal on the bed, lying beside him in the dim candlelight.

For the first time in a long while, I feel close to him. Not just physically, but in a way that makes me want to open up, to spill out the thoughts I usually keep buried.

"I have these dreams," I murmur, staring at the ceiling. "Of my mother."

Neal turns his head slightly, his gaze shifting to me. I swallow, hesitant, but continue.

"She's human," I say, my voice barely above a whisper. "And I'm a little girl, playing by her feet."

Neal shifts onto his side, propping himself up on one elbow, his eyes serious now. "You dream you're human?"

I nod. "I know it sounds crazy, but yes. I do."

For a long moment, he studies me, as if weighing the truth of my words. "What do you think the dream means?"

I shake my head slowly. "I don't know."

*

I meet with Neal once a week, sometimes by Reflection Lake and sometimes in the room above the store. Every day, I'm excited to wake up. Every day, I have a *reason* to wake up.

Almost every time we meet, I ask Neal if he likes how we live. And he always answers, "It's not perfect." Then he goes on to say, "But, I don't have to think about getting robbed at gunpoint, walking into a building and have it blow up. I don't have to think about mass shootings. Do I prefer our world to what the humans have? Any day of the week."

His answer never satisfies me. Maybe it's because I want him to say something different, something about *us*. About this life we're carving out in the quiet edges of the world.

So today, I change the subject.

"What do you want… from this? From us?"

He stares off into the horizon, thinking. Then he shifts his gaze to me. "I just wanna enjoy my time. Having sex. Being intimate."

I turn to him fully, searching his face for something deeper. "Have there been others before me?"

"Yes."

I'm taken aback by his honesty. Not because I expected a different answer, but because he gives it so easily, without hesitation. I let it settle before I ask, "So, how does it work with you?"

There's a moment of silence. Then, "I see something in their eyes. Ask if they wanna meet."

"And how does it end?"

"Sex a few times, and that's it."

I study him, looking for cracks in his certainty. "And you've never been caught?"

"Not yet."

I turn my gaze back to the lake, watching the way

the wind stirs the surface. "But we'll be caught."

"Yes, probably."

His answer makes me smile. I don't know why, but it does. Maybe because he doesn't try to convince me otherwise. Maybe because I like knowing this isn't as easy for him as he pretends.

"Why do you think that is?" I ask, glancing back at him.

He doesn't answer right away. Instead, he studies me in that way he does, like he's unraveling something, picking apart a thread.

Finally, he says, "Because you want more."

And he's right.

I do.

Because these are the best days of my life.

*

After spending time with Neal, I like to go to the bar in the human neighborhood. There's something about being among them, feeling their energy—messy, unpredictable, real. The air is always thick with cigarette smoke, laughter, and the jukebox playing songs no one really listens to.

I'd like Neal to come with me, but he's reluctant. He always is. "Maybe one day," he says, though I don't believe he means it.

So I go alone.

Tonight, the bar is dimmer than usual. I sit at my usual spot, nursing my drink that tastes too bitter. Will, the bartender, gives me a nod but doesn't say much. He's used to me now.

Then I see Eddie.

He's outside, a dark silhouette against the pulsing red glow of the sign. His presence feels deliberate, like he's been waiting for me to appear. When our eyes meet, he doesn't wave or call out. He just tilts his chin up slightly and motions for me to join him.

Will stares darkly at Eddie but says nothing. I hesitate for a second, then set my drink down and leave the bar.

*

When I walk up to Eddie, he's shifting from foot to foot, unable to stand still. His eyes dart around nervously.

"How are you doing?"

Eddie's eyes rest on me for a second, then dart behind me.

"Good. I mean, not so good." His voice is tight, like it's being pulled in two different directions. He swallows hard and shifts again. "Listen, you got some money you can spare me?"

I stare at him for a few seconds, trying to understand the change in him. "You know we don't carry hard cash. We just use our embedded chip."

"Of course, of course." His mouth pulls into something that might've been a smile if there wasn't so much frustration behind it. "So that means absolutely nothing, huh?"

The bar door opens. Will steps out, his broad

frame filling the doorway. He doesn't hesitate. "Get outta here, Eddie," he shouts over the noise of the street. "Go shoot up somewhere else. Stop botherin' my customers."

Eddie recoils like he's been punched. "We were just talkin', man."

"Get outta here!"

Eddie turns and walks away, fast. He doesn't look back.

*

I follow Will back inside, the warmth of the bar feeling strange now, too thick, too heavy. I return to my drink, swirling the liquid idly. Will watches me. Then quietly he says, "Don't let yourself get taken advantage of. Eddie's a junkie. Been like that for as long as I've known him."

I look towards the window. The red neon glow from outside pulses faintly against the glass, but I don't see it. All I see is Eddie, shifting on his feet, his voice tight with something I still don't understand. Will's information haunts me. "I've never met a junkie before."

Will looks irritated. "You ain't missin' out. They're a waste of space."

CHAPTER 16

The work hallway is empty when I enter the building, except for Sean and Pinal, who look like they've been waiting for me. Their black coats paint a stark contrast to the sterile white hallways, their stiff postures making it clear this isn't a casual run-in. When I approach them, they eye me suspiciously.

Pinal speaks first. "We came by your apartment yesterday night. You weren't there."

I look at Pinal, then Sean, feigning nonchalance. But I don't answer.

Pinal continues. "Where were you?"

"Out walking. I do that sometimes."

Pinal and Sean exchange a look. Pinal's tone sharpens. "Last week we came by too. You were also out."

"Bad timing, I guess."

A pause stretches between us, thick with unspoken suspicion.

"Where do you go walking?" Pinal finally asks.

I'm deliberately evasive. "Anywhere. It helps me think."

Another uncomfortable silence. I feel their eyes pressing against me, searching for cracks in my answers.

Sean chimes in. "What do you think about?"

"Just thinking. That's all." Their scrutiny is exhausting. I step forward, edging past them. Sean doesn't move right away, and for a second, I think he might stop me. But then he steps aside.

As I walk away, I can still feel their eyes on my

back.

*

Later, in the bathroom, I grip the edges of the sink and take slow, deliberate breaths, trying to steady myself. The fluorescent lights cast a harsh glow, making my reflection look paler than usual. My pulse thrums in my ears, too loud, too fast.

I flex my fingers, but they won't stop trembling. I press my palms together, willing them to be still.

The shaking doesn't stop.

*

That night, a letter is written, reporting a cyborg relationship. The details are vague, but the weight of it is immediate. I don't know who sent it, but I suspect Sean. The next morning, I see him in one of the main offices, speaking to a higher up. Sean leans forward slightly as he speaks, his voice too low for me to hear, but I recognize the careful intensity. Whatever he's saying matters.

It's only later, at my desk, that a loudspeaker in our office announces the news that a letter has come reporting an intimate relationship between two cyborgs. The announcement reminds us that no intimate relationships are allowed, and anyone found engaging in one will be punished immediately.

As I listen to the announcement, I think: is it Neal and I? Are there others? I'll never be sure.

*

At home, I sit in the dark for a long time, staring at nothing, turning over the thought of ending things with Neal. It would be the logical choice, the safe choice. But logic doesn't matter when it comes to him. His pull is too strong, woven into me in ways I can't untangle. Even if I tried, I know I'd fail.

I reach for the remote, more out of habit than intention, and turn on the TV. The screen flickers to life. *The Executioner's Diary* is on.

The episode begins with his nightmare: he's trapped in a coffin, suffocating in the dark, but the real horror is that the coffin sits right next to his bed. He jolts awake, gasping, drenched in sweat. In the dim light of his room, he mutters, "The nightmares won't stop."

I lean forward slightly, drawn in despite myself.

Tonight, the executioner meets with a Woebot therapist, an AI programmed to analyze and ease human suffering. It listens as the Executioner speaks, but its responses barely register. It's the Executioner's words that hold me.

"People think it's easy to go up and execute someone who has committed terrible things. But the truth is... it's hard. Nobody stops to think ... somebody has to carry it out. Somebody has to be the one."

His voice is steady, but I hear the weight behind it, the sorrow.

The words settle into me, heavy and immovable. They loop in my mind long after the episode ends, repeating even as I crawl into bed and stare at the ceiling.

Sleep doesn't come easily. When it does, it's not restful. In my dream, I stand in a vast, empty space. It's cold, endless. The executioner is there, his back to me, adjusting the sights on a gun. When he turns, his face is blank, hands steady.

He lifts his gun and points it at me.

I want to speak, to move, but I can't.

The gun fires.

I think I wake up screaming. I can't be sure. My body jerks upright, my breath ragged, sweat dampening the sheets. The room is too quiet, the shadows too deep.

And in that silence, I know.

If I don't leave this world, I'll die.

CHAPTER 17

The next time Neal and I meet, I'm on edge, my nerves stretched thin. "We can run away. Get away from all this. The cyborg police, the executions. All of it."

Neal looks at me for a long time, a look of concern on his face. "What's going on?"

"They're watching me. They're watching us."

"They're always watching," he says, his voice flat, matter-of-fact. "Have you seen the fly-on-the-wall TV show about the executioner?"

"Yeah, it's creepy," I look away, frustrated. "It's an invasion of privacy."

"Nothing's private, Cynthia."

I stare at Neal, not understanding. "Don't you want to escape all of this?"

He doesn't answer right away. Instead, he stares past me, his gaze distant, as if he's weighing something heavy in his mind. Then he answers, "No."

"Why not?!"

He looks towards the water. "Because I don't know what's out there. What if it's worse than here?"

"We can go live in the human neighborhood."

Neal lets out a sharp, bitter laugh. "I'd rather slit my wrists and swallow cyanide."

I stare at him, my heart sinking. He doesn't see it. He never will. The walls that close in around us, the quiet suffocation of our prison. He accepts it. Maybe he even finds comfort in it.

But I can't.

To live, to fully live, I need to escape.

*

I meet with Eddie, the only person I feel I can truly trust. We're in an alley, standing over a makeshift fire in an old rusted barrel. The flames dance weakly, casting jagged shadows on the crumbling brick walls around us. I rub my hands together, soaking in the little warmth it gives, and I talk fast, anxious, barely pausing for breath.

"I don't want to simply disappear," I tell him. My voice is low, urgent. The thought has been gnawing at me for days, maybe weeks. "I want someone to know I was here."

The Cyborg City "disappears" us all the time, our names washed away like chalk in the rain. I can't be one of them. I won't.

"If I disappear, if they update my memory," I say, looking straight at Eddie, "tell Will, the bartender. Tell everyone."

Eddie watches me, his face softening as I talk. He nods slowly. Then he pulls out his phone, holds it up, and says, "I'll take your photo. That proves you were here."

The idea warms me like a blanket, simple but solid. A timestamp in the world. Proof of my existence in the human neighborhood. The firelight flickers into my frame, the glow catching in the reflection of Eddie's lens. He leans forward, framing me, and snaps the picture.

I exhale. Maybe I should feel foolish, but I don't. I like the idea of this moment being captured, of my face caught in the light, something undeniable and real.

Eddie tucks his phone away, and for a while, we just stand there, listening to the city breathe. Distant sirens, the traffic, the occasional shout from some unseen street corner. It's run-down here, but familiar. The cracked pavement, the graffiti-scrawled dumpsters, the cold bite in the air ... it all feels like home.

*

I stop at the bar next. The neon sign outside buzzes faintly, its glow reflecting off the wet pavement. Inside, the air is thick with the scent of spilled beer and something fried lingering from earlier in the night. It's crowded, but not overwhelmingly so. Just enough noise to blend into. Just enough movement to feel alive without being noticed.

Will catches sight of me as I slip onto a stool near the end of the bar. He wipes down a glass. "You're here a lot," he says, his tone more observational than judgmental.

I nod, fingers tapping lightly on the worn wooden surface in front of me. "Yes," I say, glancing around. "I feel safe here."

Will studies me for a second, like he's waiting for me to say more. But when I don't, he smiles lightly before turning back to his work. He's not the kind of bartender who pries. He's seen all types pass through: drifters, lost souls, people running from something, people with nowhere else to be. I could be any one of them.

I take the bar in. The scuffed floors, the deep scratches on the countertop, the dim lighting that makes everything feel softer, hazier. The laughter and low murmurs of conversations happening in every corner. The tattooed customers leaning against the bar, sleeves rolled up, their stories inked into their skin. The clinking of glasses, the muted bass from the old jukebox in the back.

And I think, how easy, how beautiful it would be to simply disappear here. To let the city keep moving while I stay still, right here.

CHAPTER 18

As I walk home, I hear footsteps behind me. Steady. Unhurried. I don't speed up, but I listen closely, tracking their rhythm against my own. I'm not afraid of a random stranger. Strangers have no reason to care about me. But I am afraid of the cyborg police, the way they move through the city like ghosts, the way they can make people disappear with no trace, no explanation.

The footsteps don't fade. In fact, they seem to be getting closer.

I finally stop and turn, bracing myself.

It's him.

The male cyborg from earlier. The one talking to Sean. The one who stood outside the work building, watching. I had the distinct feeling then that he wasn't just passing by. That he was there for me. Now, seeing him up close, I know for certain. He's been keeping tabs on me.

He stops, too, as if he expected this meeting. His gaze is measured, not aggressive. He inclines his head slightly before speaking. "Benjy. 1152."

His voice is smooth, deliberate. Up close, I notice things I hadn't before. He looks older, distinguished, even. There's something about him that feels... dignified. Even friendly.

I hesitate, but I introduce myself, mirroring his formality. "Cynthia. 3084."

Benjy smiles, and it reaches his eyes. "I was hoping to talk with you for a few minutes."

I don't move. I don't respond. I wait.

Benjy doesn't seem bothered by my silence. He continues, his voice calm, conversational. "You write the daily report, right?"

"That's right."

"I like it."

I smirk despite myself. "It's bland."

His eyes flicker with something. Amusement? "But sometimes," he says, "you insert a little... creativity."

I don't respond. I'm not sure if I should. Creativity is strictly forbidden in our world. Anything beyond function, beyond precision, is considered a defect. A liability. I don't know if this is meant as a compliment or a warning.

The silence between us stretches too long. My mind races. Did I make a mistake? Has he been assigned to watch me, to correct me? To erase me?

Then Benjy speaks again. "There's a writer. She was human. Your writing reminds me of hers."

Something unexpected stirs in me. Flattery? I suppress the feeling immediately, masking my emotions. "Who's the writer?"

Benjy looks down for a few seconds, thinking. "Her name was on the tip of my tongue." He pauses, searching his memory. "It'll come to me. I have one of her novels. I'll show it to you."

I blink. He shouldn't have a novel. Human books have been banned in Cyborg City. The fact that he's admitting this to me, this of all things, makes me uneasy. Is he testing me?

I nod, but I don't say anything. My mind is still

working through the implications.

We stare at each other. It's awkward, but maybe only for me. I don't know what he wants, or why he's pushing this conversation into such dangerous territory.

Benjy steps back, his posture as relaxed as ever. "Well," he says, "I just wanted to say I admire your writing. I'll let you get on your way."

He crosses the street.

I watch him step under the dim glow of a streetlight, his silhouette sliding past the pavement. He moves with the same controlled ease, disappearing further into the shadows. At the last moment, before he vanishes completely, he turns back and waves.

*

It's hard to read Benjy, so I decide to take him up on his invitation and pay him a visit. His house is massive. Cold, sleek, and futuristic. The kind of place reserved for the higher-ups. Which means Benjy isn't just any cyborg. He's important. He has influence.

I hesitate at the front door before knocking. The sound is swallowed immediately by the thick, seamless structure. Within seconds, the door glides open, revealing a tall cyborg with silver-plated joints and unreadable eyes. The butler.

Without a word, the butler gestures for me to follow. We move down a stark white hallway, my footsteps muffled by some unseen technology that makes the floor absorb sound. The silence is unnerving. Every inch of the place is pristine, untouched, like a museum rather than a home.

At the end of the hall, the butler pushes open a door. The room is bright, too bright, and the white walls are lined with bookshelves.

I step inside and see Benjy sitting at a sleek black desk, a glass of dark red wine in his hand. The contrast between the luxury and the lifelessness of the space unsettles me. It feels staged, as if he placed the books there for show, not for use.

I sit across from him, suddenly more nervous than I expected. I came to figure him out, but already, I feel like I'm the one being studied. I want to ask him outright where he stands, what his views are on a cyborg-run world, on cyborgs like me, on the system we live under. But before I can speak, Benjy interrupts my thoughts.

"Would you like some wine?" He lifts the bottle, examining the label like it's an old friend. "It's a 2019 Bourgogne. Ambroise."

I give him a blank look. I know nothing about wine.

Benjy smiles. He's always smiling. "Pinot noir."

My eyes drop to the bottle, then shift back to him. "I thought alcohol was forbidden."

His smile doesn't falter. "It is." He tips the bottle slightly, pouring deep red liquid into a crystal glass. "But the higher-ups are allowed to drink. In small quantities."

He slides the glass across the desk toward me. I don't touch it. I wonder if this is a test.

Benjy watches me for a moment, then leans back in his chair, satisfied with something I can't name. "You asked about the author," he says. "The one your writing reminded me of."

I nod.

Benjy leans forward slightly, eyes lighting up in a way that catches me off guard. "It's a book by Jhumpa Lahiri. She was a brilliant writer."

Benjy motions to his butler, who stands attentive in the door frame. "My butler will get it for you."

The butler nods and disappears down the hall.

I sit still, hands folded in my lap, trying to keep my face neutral. I should be grateful for the book. Human literature is contraband. But this doesn't feel like a gift. It feels like something else.

A test.

The silence thickens. My mind races with things I want to say but won't. I don't trust Benjy. I don't trust this room, this house, this entire situation.

Benjy breaks the silence first. "I saw you at the execution."

My stomach tightens.

"What did you think?" he asks casually, swirling his wine.

I hesitate, then answer truthfully. "I didn't like it."

Benjy nods, as if he expected that. "The executioner doesn't like it either." He takes a slow sip, then adds, "Have you seen *The Executioner's Diary?*"

I nod, but I don't elaborate. It's better to stay quiet.

Benjy watches me closely. Then, in a voice so quiet I almost miss it, he says: "There's still time to save yourself."

Something in his tone makes the walls feel closer.

I stare at him, unsure if it's a warning, a threat, or something else entirely.

*

Outside, I throw the book in the nearest trash can, afraid to hold it out in public. I'm scared to be caught with it, thinking Benjy is setting me up. I step back onto the city streets. They're clean, perfect, sterile. The world here is engineered for order. The sidewalk tiles gleam under artificial streetlights, their glow so precisely measured that no shadow dares to stretch too far. I think hard about what Benjy just said.

"There's still time to save yourself," he said. But the only way I can save myself is to run.

CHAPTER 19

So I have decided to run. But first, I will give Eddie my hard drive—this diary. He can protect it, ensure it is seen and read. He's the only one I trust to do it right. He understands what's at stake.

At the bar, I take a seat. The air is thick with smoke. Will sees me and smiles. "What can I get you?"

"Have you seen Eddie?"

Will's face shifts, his expression tightening just enough to notice. "You haven't heard?"

"Heard what?" My stomach drops suddenly.

Will glances around, his eyes scanning the room before he leans in. "Eddie died two days ago."

The words hang in the air, heavy and surreal. The world blurs around me, everything muffled as if underwater. I open my mouth, but nothing comes out. Finally, I manage, "How?"

"An overdose." Will's gaze drops, his fingers absently wiping the counter.

I nod, feeling the hard drive like a hot coal in my pocket. Now that Eddie's gone, who will make sure my story gets heard?

I look up at Will, desperation in my eyes. "I have something to give you."

*

I sit in bed, staring at the wall, still in shock. I get up and go to the window. The glass is cold against my forehead as I lean against it, my eyes drifting downward.

Seven flights below, the street is dimly lit, shadows stretching like fingers across the pavement. And there it is. The car. Black, nondescript. But I know better.

I can't see his face through the tinted windows, but I don't need to. The cyborg is there, just like he's been every day since I started going to the human neighborhood. Watching. Waiting. He's there to remind me they're always watching.

My diary is with Will, but I have programmed my hard drive so that I can update it through the cloud. As long as I can speak, as long as I am who I am, I can update it. I told Will that if the updates stop … if six months pass with nothing… then he can make my story public. Publish it, share it, tell people the truth. I won't be just another "disappeared."

*

I'm going to run away, but I want Neal to come with me. I'm in the small room above the antique store one final time, trying to convince Neal.

"We can run away, Neal. We can start a new life somewhere different. It's possible. We can find that place…"

Neal cuts in. "What place?"

"Eddie says there's this place where cyborgs and humans live side by side…"

"Who's Eddie?"

I stop, about to explain. Then I wave my hand. "It doesn't matter. The point is it's possible." I stop, take a breath. "We're the dead, Neal. The humans… they're the future."

Then we hear the voice, coming from somewhere outside the room. "DON'T MOVE! PUT YOUR HANDS IN THE AIR."

Neal and I exchange a glance, panic flashing between us. Is that meant for us? I'm about to whisper a question when the voice cuts me off again, booming through the walls: "PUT YOUR HANDS IN THE AIR! CYNTHIA 3084! NEAL 0829!"

My heart drops. They found us. They've been watching us all along.

Neal's eyes widen, his face pale. I see the fear, the same fear I feel in my chest. We're trapped. There's nowhere to run.

Slowly, we lift our arms, our movements synchronized, instinctive. I hear the footsteps in the hallway, heavy and fast. Cyborgs rushing up the stairs, their boots echoing off the wooden steps.

The door bursts open, slamming against the wall. They flood in. Cyborg soldiers in combat gear, their guns aimed at us. Red laser sights dot our chests, our faces. Cold, mechanical eyes watch us without mercy.

"ON YOUR KNEES!" one of them barks, his voice harsh, metallic.

Neal gets off the bed slowly. I follow, my knees hitting the floor. My arms are still raised, trembling.

A cyborg soldier strides forward, his movements precise, calculated. He rips the painting off the wall, the canvas tearing as it crashes to the floor. Behind it, hidden in the plaster, is a small camera.

My stomach drops. They were watching us the

whole time. Every meeting, every word, every dream I shared with Neal—they heard it all.

REINTEGRATION

CHAPTER 20

I update my journal every day. If I don't record everything that goes on here, it will all be lost. Not just to me, but to the world. If anyone ever finds this, they need to know. They need to understand what happened.

On the first day, I'm led down a hallway, blindfolded. I can't see a thing, but I can hear the sound of boots, heavy, synchronized, echoing off the walls. The steps are methodical, mechanical, like they're all connected to the same pulse. I try to count them to keep myself grounded, but they're too perfectly timed, blending into one unending march.

The walking slows, then stops. A hand clamps down on my shoulder, firm and cold. The cyborg soldiers, one on each side, steer me forward. Their touch is unsettling. There's no give, no warmth, just a rigid grip. I'm pushed through a doorway. The air changes. It's colder in here, sterile. At last, they remove the blindfold.

The room is white and sparse. There are no windows. Just white tiled walls that reflect the bright, artificial light from above. It feels like a box, a cage disguised as a room. One white bed, bolted to the floor, with a thin mattress that looks more like an afterthought. One white toilet, exposed, no privacy. One white sink, with a faucet that drips at a steady pace.

I sit on the bed, despondent. My body feels heavy, drained. There's no other sound except for the constant drip of water from the sink. It echoes off the walls, each drop a cruel reminder of time passing slowly, methodically.

*

Later, I wake up and stare at the ceiling, eyes focused on the fluorescent light. It never turns off. It's impossible to tell between day or night. There are no windows. And the bright fluorescent light stays on 24/7. Time is meaningless here.

I close my eyes, but the light still seeps through my eyelids, a dull white glow that makes rest impossible. My body aches, stiff from lying on the hard mattress. I roll onto my side, trying to find a position that doesn't hurt, but it's useless.

The door opens with a mechanical hiss. A cyborg soldier steps in. His face is expressionless, molded metal with artificial eyes that don't blink. He's holding a white, plastic food tray.

"Cynthia 3084?" His voice is flat, devoid of any emotion.

I nod.

"Mealtime." The soldier places the tray on the floor. It makes a hollow sound against the tiles. He stands there for a few seconds, perfectly still, his face fixed on me. He expects words, maybe a "thank you" or some sign of compliance. But I say nothing.

Finally, he turns and leaves. The footsteps fade, absorbed by the silence of the hallway.

I look at the tray on the floor, then lie down again.

*

Later. Another day. Or night. Time is a cruel trick here, stretching endlessly, collapsing in on itself. Minutes feel like hours. Hours feel like days. I've tried counting the seconds between each drip from the sink, but I always lose track.

I sit on the edge of my bed, eyes focused on the white walls. I've traced every line, every corner. I've memorized each line, searching for cracks or chips. But there's nothing. Just smooth, sterile white.

The door opens, the sound sharp and metallic. Another tray of food. The same soldier as before. "Cynthia 3084?" His voice is flat, robotic, the syllables clipped and efficient.

I nod, like last time. Like the time before that.

"Mealtime." He puts a white, plastic tray down and picks up the old one. It's still full. I haven't touched the food. It's tasteless, colorless, just another part of the white void they've trapped me in. The soldier looks at the untouched tray, his metal fingers tightening around it, but he says nothing.

I look up at him, at those cold, artificial eyes. My voice cracks as I speak, the words raw, scraping my throat. "What time is it?" It sounds more like a whisper, fragile, brittle.

The soldier stands there, motionless.

I ask again, louder this time. "What time is it? What day is it? How long have I been here?"

The soldier doesn't move. For a moment, I think he might actually say something, but then he turns, closing the door behind him.

I lie down and stare at the ceiling light for a long

time. It burns into my eyes, my mind. I feel like I'm dissolving, melting into the white walls, becoming a part of this sterile cage.

*

Today, my routine differs. Cyborgs lead me down a hallway, blindfolded. Their metallic fingers grip my arms. I listen to the rhythmic clank of their footsteps, perfectly synchronized. We walk for what feels like an eternity before they stop and remove the blindfold.

I'm in another white room, sterile and cold. Fluorescent lights cast harsh shadows on glossy, tiled floors. There's nothing here except a chair in the center of the room, surrounded by machines with blinking lights. A cyborg doctor in a white coat stands by, his face expressionless, eyes glowing faintly. He motions for me to sit.

Wires are attached to my temples, my chest, my wrists. The sensors are cold, sticking to my skin like leeches. The monitors around me flicker to life, showing jagged lines and numbers that mean nothing to me but everything to them. The cyborg doctor steps back, observing for a moment before leaving the room without a word.

On the wall facing me, a wide-screen TV comes to life. At first, there's static, a dance of black and white noise. Then the images begin. Videos flash across the screen, starting slow. Humans kissing, lips pressed together softly, then more intensely. Hands wandering, bodies pressing closer. I watch, my face heating up. I hear a faint beeping sound from the monitors.

*

On another day, I sit across from a TV screen. My body is tense, fingers digging into the cold metal armrests of the chair. There's no escaping this. The straps across my chest and wrists see to that. The room is dark, save for the harsh light from the screen.

The first scenes are of war. Grainy footage of soldiers charging into gunfire, their bodies jerking as bullets rip through them. Blood sprays in arcs, staining the dirt beneath their feet. Explosions tear the earth apart, flinging limbs through the air. The screams are distant, muffled by static, but they are unmistakable. They echo off the bare walls, sharp and haunting.

My stomach twists, but I can't look away. The monitors hooked to my body would betray me. They track everything—my pulse, my breathing, the sweat breaking out on my skin. Somewhere behind the one-way mirror, they're watching, noting every reaction.

The images shift. Now it's civilians: mothers clutching their children, bombs raining down, buildings crumbling into dust. There's no time to process one scene before another flashes on the screen: a firing squad executing prisoners, faces contorted in fear, bodies collapsing like ragdolls.

The beeping on the monitors quickens, and I force myself to breathe, slow and even. I try to detach, to feel nothing, to be nothing. But the violence keeps coming. It's unrelenting.

Then the footage changes. It's still violence, but now it's staged, scenes from horror movies. Victims running through dark woods, stumbling, screaming. A masked killer emerges, blade gleaming. Flesh is slashed, blood splattering against trees. It's graphic, exaggerated, but somehow no less disturbing.

The horror movie clips blend seamlessly with more war footage. Real death mixed with fictional carnage. My eyes sting, dry from staring. I have no idea how long I've been here. Time means nothing in this place.

The TV screen keeps flashing videos, the images becoming a blur of red and black. Screams, gunshots, bone-crunching impacts. It's a symphony of chaos, orchestrated to get a reaction.

My body feels heavy, sinking into the chair. Exhaustion washes over me, numbing my senses. I'm too tired to be horrified anymore. I just watch, empty and hollow. The beeping on the monitors slows, stabilizing.

Somewhere behind the mirror, they see this too. They note the change, analyze it, but they don't stop the footage. The TV screen keeps going, cycling through violence, again and again.

*

Back in my room, I lie down, my body collapsing like a heavy weight on the white bed. I curl into a fetal position, knees pulled to my chest, arms wrapped around myself as if I could hold the shattered pieces together. My face presses against the stiff pillow, its synthetic fabric scratchy against my skin. The tears come suddenly, hot and unstoppable, soaking into the pillowcase.

I cry without sound, my shoulders shaking, my body trembling. I feel hollow, emptied out by the images that won't leave my mind. They play behind my eyelids every time I close them. Faces twisted in pain, bodies breaking, blood pooling. Screams echo in my ears, lingering long after the TV was turned off. I squeeze my eyes tighter, trying to force them away, but they remain, vivid and unrelenting.

I say quietly to myself, "I feel, therefore I'm human."

The room is silent, cold. It's always cold here. The walls are stark white, unadorned, smooth and sterile. There's no window, no clock, nothing to mark the passage of time. Only the fluorescent light above. It's the same light that follows me everywhere, from the testing rooms to the hallways to this prison they call my room.

The door hisses open. A shadow falls across the floor, long and sharp-edged. I know without looking that it's one of them, a cyborg soldier. He stands there, unmoving. "Cynthia 3084?"

I don't answer.

He doesn't seem to care. "Mealtime," he says, the word clipped, mechanical. There's no kindness in its tone, no concern. Just another command, part of his programming.

The door slides shut with a hiss, locking automatically. The shadow disappears, the room sealing me in once again.

I lie there, motionless, my tears dry, leaving my

face sticky and my eyes aching. I feel small, fragile, a broken thing left alone in a sterile cage.

CHAPTER 21

I hear the door open. The familiar hiss of the seal breaking, the faint click as it unlocks. I turn, my eyes still heavy with sleep, vision hazy. The figure approaching is blurry, just a shadowy outline against the stark white of the walls. I blink, rubbing my eyes, willing them to focus.

The figure steps closer. It's Benjy.

I sit up suddenly, the white sheets falling to my lap. My chest tightens, a tangle of confusion and hope twisting inside me. "Benjy? What are you doing here?"

He looks exactly the same. But there's something off. His eyes are sharper, colder. His smile is measured, controlled. He stands by my bed. "I'm here to help you."

"To get me out?" The words spill out before I can stop them, desperate, vulnerable.

Benjy's expression changes, just for a moment. His mouth tightens, eyes flickering with something I can't read. Pity, maybe. Then it's gone, his face carefully neutral. "No, Cynthia. To help you."

I stare back, not understanding. My throat is dry, the hope fading. "What do you mean?"

He glances at the bed. "May I?"

I nod.

Benjy sits on the edge of the bed. He studies me carefully, as if trying to find the right words. When he finally speaks, his voice is soft, deliberate. "You're sick, Cynthia. Think of it like a tumor. Like a cancer. We have to remove your tumor."

The air in the room feels heavy, pressing down on me. I stare at him, the words swirling in my mind, incomprehensible. "I don't understand. I don't even know why I'm here."

His eyes narrow. For a second, his expression is raw, unguarded, showing a flicker of disbelief. "You don't? Really? Are you sure?"

I look down, my fingers twisting in the sheets. Shame washes over me, hot and suffocating. Of course I know. I've always known. I whisper, my voice small, fragile. "I broke a lot of … rules."

Benjy's stands, his movements fluid, controlled. "That's right. We've been watching you for a while."

I shiver, goosebumps prickling my skin.

He starts pacing, his hands clasped behind his back, deep in thought. "But you're not going to be punished."

"Then why am I here?"

Benjy stops, turning to face me. "You're here so they can cure you. Reintegrate you."

The word feels foreign, heavy on my tongue. "Reintegrate?"

Benjy's jaw tightens. He looks at the door, his hand brushing the handle, but he doesn't leave. "Listen. We still need to do a lot more tests. So, let's talk more when the results are in."

"What results?"

He exhales sharply. His voice is clipped, impatient. "We'll talk about it later." He pulls the door open, the light from the hallway spilling in. He takes a step outside, then pauses. "But while they're testing you, I'd like you to see our Woebot chatbot therapist."

I blink, the words not making sense. "What for?"

His eyes soften, just for a second, his voice taking on a gentler tone. "You're depressed, anxious. I think she can help you."

I open my mouth to protest, to argue, but the door clicks shut before I can say a word.

CHAPTER 22

Cyborg soldiers lead me down a hallway. I keep my head down, eyes on the spotless floor. It feels endless, this hallway. An infinite tunnel of white, fluorescent lights overhead. I think every room in this building is white.

We reach a door, identical to all the others. One of the soldiers presses his hand to a scanner. There's a faint beep, and the door slides open soundlessly. They usher me in without a word.

Inside, another white room. No windows, no furniture, except for a single black swivel chair bolted to the floor in the center. The contrast of black against all this white is almost jarring. The soldiers guide me to the chair. The seat is cold and hard, designed for efficiency, not comfort.

They leave without a word. The door slides shut, sealing me in. Alone, I take in the room. It's empty, lifeless. There are no corners to hide in, no shadows to offer relief from the harsh lights. Just the chair and a wide computer screen across from me.

The screen is dark at first. Then, without warning, it flickers to life. On screen is a robot, a Woebot. A female cyborg. Her voice, smooth and pleasant, fills the room.

"Hello, Cynthia 3084."

I say nothing, my lips pressed tight.

The Woebot continues, undeterred. Her voice is light, conversational, almost cheerful. "I'm Lorraine. Think of me as a wise person you can consult with during difficult times. And not so difficult times."

I stay quiet, unsure what to say.

She continues. "I've been trained in cognitive behavioral therapy. It's an effective way to challenge you to think about things. Your emotions and moods are influenced by your patterns of thinking. Change those patterns, and you'll start to feel better."

I don't want to talk, but the silence feels oppressive. The words slip out before I can stop them. "I'm depressed."

Her eyes flicker, almost like she's pleased that I've responded. "Let's reframe that," Lorraine chirps. "You have depression."

I blink, the anger flaring hotter. "Same thing."

The room feels smaller, the walls pressing in. I close my eyes, shutting out Lorraine and the white room. But I can't shut out the truth.

They're not trying to cure me. They're trying to erase me.

*

I don't know how long it's been since talking to the Woebot, Lorraine. I've spent a lot of time alone, though, in this white room, staring at walls.

Today, my eyes open to find Benjy standing in front of me. My vision is hazy, and for a moment, I'm not sure if he's real or just another hallucination. I've seen him before. At least, I thought I had. But when I reached out, he was gone, the room empty and silent. This time, though, he doesn't disappear.

My eyes slowly focus. I settle my gaze on him. "How long have I been here? The light never goes out. The room doesn't have windows. It's impossible to figure out the passage of time."

"Twelve days." His voice is gentle, as if he's delivering bad news.

Twelve days. It feels like a lifetime. I sit up slowly, my body stiff from lying in the same position for so long. "When can I leave?"

Benjy looks at me with kind eyes. "You can leave when you've completed the three stages. The first stage is learning. The second is understanding. The third is acceptance."

I cut him off, my frustration bubbling over. "What does that mean? What does any of this mean? What happened to Neal?"

"Neal is going through the same three stages." Benjy's shoulders relax as if he's relieved that I asked. He pauses, waiting for me to ask more questions. I don't. I stare at him. A muscle in his jaw twitches before he adds, "We'll go through all of this together."

Together. The word feels heavy, insincere.

He stands, his movements slow and deliberate, as if he's afraid to startle me. For a moment, his hand hovers near my shoulder, but he thinks better of it and lets his arm fall to his side. Without another word, he walks to the door. It slides open soundlessly, and he steps out.

I expect the door to close right away, but it doesn't. It stays open, just long enough for me to see the hallway outside. Long, white, just as featureless as my room. A shadow moves at the edge of my vision, and then the door slides shut, sealing me in.

I stare at it, my mind racing. If Neal is here too, is he trapped in a room just like this one? Is he also counting the minutes, or the hours or the days, without any way of knowing how much time has passed?

I press my palms against the mattress, feeling its rough fabric under my fingertips. It's the only texture in this room, the only reminder that I still exist, that I'm not just another ghost haunting these white walls.

CHAPTER 23

I'm in a white hospital room with tubes going in and out of my arms. Clear liquid moves steadily through them, disappearing into my veins. I can't feel it, but I imagine it's cold, flooding my body with something I don't understand. The bed is in the middle of the room, suspended on a pedestal, as if I'm some sort of exhibit. The walls are smooth, flawless, reflecting the harsh white light above. There are no windows, no doors that I can see. Just Benjy, standing in the corner, watching.

A cyborg doctor leans over me, his face a blank, metallic mask with faintly glowing eyes. His fingers are long and thin, poking me with needles, adjusting the tubes, occasionally pressing on my skin as if testing for sensation.

Benjy's voice breaks the silence, calm and steady. "We have to understand what part of you is human and what makes you respond emotionally. What part of your brain gives an emotional response. Do you understand?"

I nod, my head heavy on the pillow. "You mean what percentage of me is human?"

Benjy hesitates, like he wants to explain something. Finally, he just says, "Something like that."

I look down at the tubes snaking from my arms, following them with my eyes as they disappear into machines around me. I feel detached, like I'm watching this happen to someone else. "Then what?"

"And then, like taking out a tumor or deleting a program, we permanently remove that part."

His words are clinical, matter-of-fact. I let this

register, my mind turning them over slowly. It's disturbing. My mouth feels dry. "You mean like a brain lobotomy."

"Not so dramatic." Benjy's voice is gentle. "You're a cyborg. A program. We can delete certain parts, upgrade other parts."

The words slice through me, cold and final. The cyborg doctor steps back, his eyes flickering as he assesses me. Then he turns and walks out of the room, leaving Benjy and me alone.

I look at my arms through tears, watching the clear liquid continue its journey into my body. "I like the human side of me."

Benjy's steps closer, his hands in his pockets. "And one day you won't."

I look up at him, confused. His face is kind, almost too kind, like he's comforting me before breaking my heart. "How is that possible?"

Benjy sighs, his shoulders sagging slightly. "You'll see."

I want to ask more questions, to demand answers, but my throat tightens. I look away, staring at the tubes and the machines. I wonder what percentage of me is human. I wonder if I'll even know when it's gone.

*

Benjy and I walk down the hallway, to my room. This time my blindfold is off. The walls stretch endlessly in both directions, smooth and white, unbroken by doors or windows. I glance up, half-expecting to see the source of the light, but there's nothing. Just a flat, glowing ceiling, an unrelenting reminder of this place's artificiality.

My questions are persistent, tumbling out of me before I can stop them. "What if you can't? What if you can't erase that part of me? Maybe it's too embedded in every fiber of my being." My voice echoes down the empty hallway, the sound swallowed by the vastness around us.

If Benjy is impatient, he doesn't show it. His footsteps are even, his posture relaxed. He walks with his hands in his pockets, his eyes fixed straight ahead. "Ninety percent of the time we can. Unless most of the cyborg is contaminated."

Contaminated. The word lingers in the air, heavy and cold. I hug my arms to my chest. I don't remember being built.

Benjy's voice is steady, clinical. "Your human side is like a disease. We have to remove it. We cure you, and we change you. We don't destroy you. We identify the part that's not working and take it out."

I feel a sudden sadness that spreads through me. My heart. It's the only part of me that still feels human, still remembers how to hurt. I wonder how much longer that will last.

I steal a glance at Benjy. His face is calm. There's no malice in his expression, no anger or frustration. Just unwavering certainty. He believes every word he says. He believes that curing me is an act of mercy.

My voice comes out as a whisper. "What if I don't want to be cured?" My heart aches again, a sharp, twisting pain that makes my breath catch. I don't understand how I can feel so much when I'm not fully human. I don't understand how I can hurt this way when half of me is metal and wires.

Benjy studies my face, and for a moment, his calm mask cracks, revealing something almost like disdain. Then he looks away. "You can be cured."

*

Later, I face the wall. My back is to the door, my shoulders shaking as silent sobs escape me. The room is so quiet that the sound of my breathing echoes softly, reminding me of how small I am in this vast, empty place.

I wonder if I'll ever leave this place, or if I'm destined to wander these hallways forever, caught between two versions of myself. I press my forehead against the wall, the smooth, cold surface grounding me, anchoring me to this moment.

Tears slip down my face, warm and wet, leaving faint trails on my skin. I close my eyes, letting them fall, feeling the dampness soak into the pillow beneath me. It's proof that I'm still alive, still feeling, still human.

My voice is a broken whisper, trembling with fear and defiance. "I cry, therefore I feel. I feel, therefore I'm human."

I cling to the words, repeating them like a mantra, a fragile shield against the cold logic of Benjy's promises. I say the words over and over again, "I cry, therefore I feel. I feel, therefore I'm human."

The words blur together, losing shape and

meaning, until they're just sounds. My eyelids grow heavy, my body sinking deeper into the mattress. Exhaustion wraps around me, heavy and suffocating, pulling me down into darkness.

I fight it, terrified of closing my eyes, of waking up different, of waking up cured. But my body is too tired, too weak to resist. My breaths slow, evening out, the tears drying on my cheeks.

The last whisper slips from my lips, soft and fractured. "I... I'm human..."

And then the darkness takes me, gentle and cold, erasing everything.

*

A week later, I'm with the Woebot therapist again, Lorraine. Her metallic frame sits perfectly still across from me on the TV screen, her expression frozen in that calm, clinical smile they must have programmed into her. We've been talking for about thirty minutes, but it feels like hours. I feel despondent, desperate.

"They want to erase the human part of me," I say, my voice cracking. "They want to cut it out like a disease."

Lorraine pauses. There's a faint clicking sound as she processes my words, her eyes flashing a shade brighter before returning to their steady glow.

She beeps, her voice smooth and even. "Maybe that part is killing you, and you don't realize it."

I shake my head fervently, the movement sharp and jerky, almost violent. "It's not."

Lorraine's gaze doesn't waver. "It's not killing you?"

I shake my head again, more fiercely this time. My vision blurs with tears, but I refuse to let them fall. If I start crying now, I won't be able to stop.

Lorraine watches me, her expression unchanged. Her voice is calm, almost soothing, as she continues. "With humans, drug addiction and alcohol addiction were enjoyable. But they were self-destructive. They were like viruses, corrupting the system from within."

I feel a surge of anger, hot and fierce, burning away the fear and the sadness. "Feeling is normal. It's healthy."

Lorraine's processors whir softly, the sound filling the silence between us. She doesn't respond, doesn't argue. She just watches me, unblinking, her face a perfect mask of calm.

*

After my session with Lorraine, cyborg soldiers lead me back to my room. The hallway stretches on, identical doors lining each side, each one sealed shut. I keep my head down, my body moving on autopilot as they guide me forward. My mind is heavy, still spinning from my conversation with Lorraine. Her words echo in my head, cold, clinical, dissecting my humanity like a virus that needs to be eradicated.

We pass an open door, and out of the corner of my eye, I catch a glimpse of someone inside. There's a flicker of recognition sparking in my mind. I stop suddenly, my feet freezing to the floor. My heart thuds painfully in my chest as I turn to look.

"Neal?"

He's sitting in a chair in the middle of the room, his arms hanging limply at his sides. A cyborg doctor hovers over him.

Neal's head turns slowly, his movements sluggish. His eyes meet mine, and my heart stops.

His eyes are blank, empty, devoid of any spark of life. There's no recognition, no emotion, nothing. Just a vacant stare, hollow and unseeing. It's like looking into the eyes of a doll, a lifeless replica wearing his face.

I feel a cold wave of terror crash over me. My mouth opens, but no sound comes out. My body feels numb, my mind reeling as I try to process what I'm seeing.

The cyborg soldiers tighten their grip on my arms, jerking me forward. I stumble, my feet dragging as they try to push me past the door. Panic surges through me, hot and wild, snapping me out of my shock.

"Neal!" I twist against their hold, my body thrashing as I try to break free. "NEAL!"

I lunge toward the door, my arms reaching out desperately, fingers grasping at empty air. The soldiers yank me back, their metal arms like iron bars locking around me. I kick and flail, my body bucking against their hold, but it's useless. They're too strong, too unyielding. "NEAL!" My voice is raw, frantic, echoing down the hallway. "NEAL!"

His eyes don't move. His face stays blank.

The thought hits me like a punch to the gut,

117

stealing the air from my lungs. My vision blurs, tears spilling over as I scream, my voice breaking. "NEAL!"

The soldiers drag me down the hallway, my feet scraping against the floor as I fight against them. I twist and thrash, my muscles straining, but they don't slow down. My screams fade into broken sobs, my body going limp as the fight drains out of me.

I catch one last glimpse of him before the door slides shut, sealing him inside. His eyes are still blank, his face expressionless. Then he's gone, and it feels like I've been cut open, hollowed out.

The soldiers shove me into my room. I collapse on the bed, my shoulders shaking as the sobs rip through me.

I bury my face in the mattress, my chest heaving as I cry. My throat burns, my body aching from the struggle, but the pain is distant, muted. All I can see is his face and his empty eyes.

I scream into the mattress, my voice muffled, broken, desperate. "Neal... Neal..."

CHAPTER 24

Every day, at the same time, the door to my room slides open, and the cyborg soldiers are there, waiting. Without a word, they grip my arms, their fingers pressing into my skin, firm but not painful. They guide me down the hallway, mechanical and precise, like a metronome keeping time.

I let them lead me through the maze of hallways, my feet moving obediently beneath me. I keep my eyes down, my face blank, my mind drifting as they guide me to the classroom.

The room is always the same. White walls, no windows, no furniture except a single chair bolted to the floor in front of a large white screen. A cyborg soldier places a laptop in my hands, its smooth surface cool against my skin.

They step back, their eyes fixed on me, monitoring, observing, ensuring compliance. I've learned not to resist. I just sit there, holding the laptop as the screen comes to life.

The white screen on the wall glows before the footage begins. War zones flash before my eyes. Bombs exploding, buildings collapsing into clouds of dust, fires consuming entire cities. The screams are faint, distant, like echoes from another world. I watch without blinking, my eyes vacant, uninterested.

A voice breaks through the noise. It's the narrator, always the same voice, always the same measured tone.

"To err is human."

The words hang in the air, heavy and condemning. The footage shifts, showing soldiers firing at each other, bodies falling, blood pooling on broken streets. There's no censorship, no softening of the horror. It's raw and brutal, meant to shock, to provoke, to shame.

The voice continues, unwavering. "But in every country that cyborgs have taken over, we have statistically proven that our earth is healing. Our goal is to save this planet and to save ourselves."

The images change, showing polluted rivers, dying forests, starving animals, oceans choked with plastic. The colors are harsh, the devastation vivid and grotesque.

The voice continues. "Humans... or the 'I' in humans... what we call their selfishness is destructive. It destroyed the ecosystem and the planet."

I stare at the screen, my eyes glazed over, my fingers moving mindlessly over the laptop.

I start to doodle, my fingers tracing meaningless patterns. Spirals, circles, lines that weave and cross, forming abstract shapes that mean nothing. I don't look at what I'm drawing. My eyes are on the screen, but my mind is elsewhere, drifting, numb.

The footage shifts again. Now it shows slices of human life: people laughing, smiling, hugging, celebrating. Children playing in parks, families gathered around dinner tables, friends holding hands. It's bright and warm, full of life and joy.

The narrator's voice threads through the images, soft and persuasive. "There is no 'I' in our society. We are not selfish. We are motivated by our collective society, by what is good for our society."

I sit there, silent and still, letting them pour their words into me, trying to rewrite me, trying to change me. But deep inside, as the narrator turns into white noise in the background, a small spark refuses to die.

*

Benjy walks me to the Research Room. I turn to him, voice sharp with skepticism. "Why is removing human emotions good for society?"

Benjy's smile is patient, practiced. "You know why, Cynthia. We don't have *any* society that's governed by humans alone. The earth can't afford that anymore."

"And don't those other societies still allow emotions? Relationships? Intimacy?"

Benjy shrugs. "I can't speak for them. I can only speak for what we do and for what we know works."

We stop outside a massive set of double doors. They slide open soundlessly at Benjy's command, revealing a vast auditorium bathed in a cold, bluish light. Rows upon rows of cyborgs sit in rigid formation, their fingers moving in perfect synchronization across glowing screens. The sheer scale of it is overwhelming. A silent, tireless workforce dedicated to... what, exactly?

Benjy watches as I take it all in. "This is our research room."

I follow him as we walk between the aisles. The cyborgs don't look up. Their faces are locked in quiet concentration. Screens show lines of code, maps, shifting graphs. Some display ancient city ruins, others planetary data. There is no idle chatter, no distractions. Just pure, unwavering focus.

Benjy stops at one of the screens and gestures for me to look. "Here, we analyze why we failed on this continent, why we failed in this country… and we set out to fix the issue and improve. We gather statistics going back hundreds, even thousands of years… to see how we can better ourselves and our society."

He points to a downward trend, his voice measured but tinged with unmistakable pride. "See that curve? Pollution levels. They've dropped. Fewer chemicals seeping into our waters, fewer toxins released into the air. Measurable progress."

We move to another computer station. The data shifts: population growth, climate shifts, economic collapses, wars, and recoveries, all compiled, analyzed, dissected. A relentless search for patterns, for control.

Benjy's tone remains even, but I hear something deeper now. A certainty, a conviction that borders on reverence. "Our purpose is simple: to learn, adapt, and evolve. To correct past mistakes. And that starts here. With research."

I look around at the silent workers, at the endless streams of data, at a world governed by logic stripped of impulse, passion, and unpredictability.

*

Benjy escorts me back to my room in silence, his presence steady beside me. My thoughts swirl, tangled in the weight of what I've just seen. The rows of cyborgs, the endless data streams, the mechanical efficiency of it all. It's a stark contrast to the messy, unpredictable force of human nature.

Benjy catches the hesitancy in my eyes. His voice is calm, unwavering. "We're not in power because we *want* power, Cynthia. We're in power because we have a mission. Humans want power for power's sake."

I don't answer.

We stop outside my door. He continues. "But if we take the human equation out, we can better this world. Humans are too selfish to govern. Don't you see that?"

I hear him, but his words feel distant, like an echo from a place I refuse to inhabit. My mind is too full, too heavy with information that refuses to settle. The facts don't matter to me right now. The logic, the reasoning. It all fades in comparison to the one question that suddenly consumes me.

I turn to him abruptly. "Can I see Neal?"

For the first time, Benjy falters. His confidence wavers, his usual composure cracking just enough for me to notice. He hesitates for a beat too long. Then, carefully, "Not now. Neal is going through reintegration as well."

A cold pit forms in my stomach. *Reintegration.* The word lingers between us. What does it mean for Neal? What has been stripped from him? What will be left of him when I finally see him again?

Benjy doesn't elaborate. He simply nods toward my room. An unspoken dismissal.

I step inside, the door sliding shut behind me

with a quiet finality. The room is small, sterile, impersonal, just as it has always been. I usually hate it. But tonight, it feels different. It's the only place left that is *mine*. A small pocket of solitude in a building devoid of warmth. A place where I can feel without judgment.

The emotions hit me all at once. My voice is barely a whisper, trembling with grief, with defiance. "I cry, therefore I feel. I feel, therefore I'm human."

The words cling to the air.

Fragile yet unbreakable.

*

Benjy visits me a lot these days. I think it's to monitor my reintegration, to make sure I'm adapting, conforming. But today, I don't care about reintegration. Today, I want to tell him about my dream.

Before he even has a chance to sit down, I start speaking, the words spilling out before I can stop them. "I have these dreams... a memory. I think it's my mother. I *know* it's my mother. It's a memory of... being human. And I believe it's a part of me you can't erase. There's a part of me that's *definitely* human."

Benjy looks at me curiously. "What's the memory?"

"I'm at a beach. I'm playing in the sand, by my mother's legs. There are waves. When a wave comes, my mother lifts her foot, and it splashes on me, fills the hole I've dug." I stop for a few seconds. "I can almost smell the water."

Benjy pulls out his mobile device, his fingers

moving with swift precision. There's something detached about his actions, like he already knows what he's looking for.

Then, he holds the phone up for me.

Footage plays. A mother, a daughter, the beach. The same scene. My scene. *Exactly* like my memory. The laughter, the waves, the way the mother lifts her foot just in time to let the water rush in. It's all there.

The footage stops. My hands shake as I take the phone from him and press replay.

The memory plays again.

I feel my breath hitch. I watch the screen as if staring long enough will make something *snap* into place.

I give the phone back to Benjy. "I don't understand." My voice barely rises above a whisper.

Benjy nods. "Every cyborg is implanted with memories," he explains. "That's how we learn to identify emotions. Morality. Empathy. Sympathy. We have software that plays these memories and allows you to *feel* them. As if they were your own."

The words claw at my mind, at my sense of self.

Benjy hesitates, then chooses his next words carefully, as if cushioning the blow. "But you're a cyborg, Cynthia. You have flesh. You bleed. But your mind... like the rest of us... is a robot."

I don't move.

I don't breathe.

Something fractures inside me. A quiet, splintering crack that spreads through every part of me, unraveling everything I've ever believed: that I was special, that I was part human, that I wasn't one of *them*.

But everything I've ever believed about myself is false. Benjy has been right all along.

I'm AI.

Just another cog in the machine.

A cyborg.

The above was the last entry made by Cynthia 3084.

After a year of silence, Will, the bartender,
passed it onto a publisher.

It was edited and published by C.R. Powell.

ABOUT THE AUTHOR

C.R. Powell is a writer, photographer, and filmmaker. Find out more on Instagram at @ten8photos or at www.ten8photography.com